"It's danger

Rio sank onto the ~~bed~~ ped her shoulders.

She turned to face him, her hair trailing across his wrists. "A lot of things are dangerous, cowboy."

Dropping her gaze to Rio's sensuous mouth, she ran her tongue along her bottom lip. Could they just share one kiss that wasn't a fake or didn't get interrupted?

Rio curled his hand around her neck. "You like playing with fire, don't you?"

"Let's just say I'll do what it takes to get my son back."

"How do you know you can trust me?" He dropped his thumb to the hollow of her throat and she swallowed.

"Because I've been stark naked under this robe since I got out of the shower, and you've hardly made a move."

CAROL ERICSON

A SILVERHILL CHRISTMAS

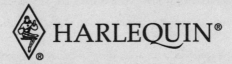

HARLEQUIN®

TORONTO • NEW YORK • LONDON
AMSTERDAM • PARIS • SYDNEY • HAMBURG
STOCKHOLM • ATHENS • TOKYO • MILAN • MADRID
PRAGUE • WARSAW • BUDAPEST • AUCKLAND

For my Uncle Frank, a nonagenarian inspiration.

Recycling programs
for this product may
not exist in your area.

ISBN-13: 978-0-373-69517-1

A SILVERHILL CHRISTMAS

ABOUT THE AUTHOR

Carol Ericson lives with her husband and two sons in Southern California, home of state-of-the-art cosmetic surgery, wild freeway chases, palm trees bending in the Santa Ana winds and a million amazing stories. These stories, along with hordes of virile men and feisty women, clamor for release from Carol's head. It makes for some interesting headaches until she sets them free to fulfill their destinies and her readers' fantasies. To find out more about Carol, her books and her strange headaches, please visit her website at www.carolericson.com, "where romance flirts with danger."

Books by Carol Ericson

HARLEQUIN INTRIGUE

1034—THE STRANGER AND I
1079—A DOCTOR-NURSE ENCOUNTER
1117—CIRCUMSTANTIAL MEMORIES
1184—THE SHERIFF OF SILVERHILL
1231—THE McCLINTOCK PROPOSAL
1250—A SILVERHILL CHRISTMAS

Don't miss any of our special offers. Write to us at the following address for information on our newest releases.

Harlequin Reader Service
U.S.: 3010 Walden Ave., P.O. Box 1325, Buffalo, NY 14269
Canadian: P.O. Box 609, Fort Erie, Ont. L2A 5X3

CAST OF CHARACTERS

Tori Scott—The ex-wife of Mad Prince Alexi of Glazkova, Tori is ready to make a move to reclaim her son. She's prepared to engage the services of one of the McClintock brothers from her hometown of Silverhill, but when the McClintock in question turns out to be illegitimate brother Rio McClintock, Tori must balance her attraction for Rio with her determination to rescue her son.

Rio McClintock—The black sheep of the McClintock family, Rio has carved out his own place in the world without the McClintocks. When a sexy princess needs his help to rescue her son from a criminal, how can Rio refuse her? Even if it means facing the family who rejected him.

Prince Alexi Zherkov—The pampered prince of the small country of Glazkova turned to drug trafficking to maintain his lifestyle. Now he wants his princess back and he's willing to use their son to get her.

Vladimir Kolchenko—He's known as the "White Russian," and his presence in Maui with Prince Alexi indicates that this trip is more business than pleasure.

Grant Swain—A small-time drug dealer in Maui is about to hit the big time. Is this opportunity his ticket to paradise or a one-way trip to the morgue?

Ivan Batalova—Ordered to keep watch over Tori while she's with her son, he's loyal to his prince and is trained to kill anyone who attempts to take the future prince.

Irina Popov—Maksim's nanny, she's been Tori's eyes and ears. If Prince Alexi finds out about her betrayal, she'll lose more than her job.

Maksim Zherkov—Tori's son hasn't seen his mother in two years. Will he leave with her willingly, or will his father groom him for a life of crime?

Chapter One

Rio McClintock dug his elbows into the moist, volcanic dirt, cursed the CIA and adjusted his binoculars. He focused on the terrace, decked out in Christmas lights, hanging over the inky Pacific. A crush of people mingled, sipping expensive booze and congratulating themselves on their good luck. He could almost hear the tinkling glasses and murmur of voices from his perch.

Another party. Didn't those people have anything better to do than eat, drink and be merry?

And didn't they realize their generous host, Mad Prince Alexi, supplied arms and ammunition to a motley crew of terrorists and two-bit dictators the world over?

The sea of people parted as a tall man, dressed in dark slacks and a black turtleneck, cut a swath through the patio. Alexi looked like a black hawk descending on a field of brightly colored birds of paradise.

Who the hell wore black in Hawaii? Rio ran a finger along the neckline of his sweat-soaked black T-shirt. Unless you had to.

He rolled onto his side and dug one of two water bottles out of his backpack, avoiding his Colt .45. Leaning on one elbow, he chugged half the bottle and then ground it into the thick carpet of mulch that cushioned his lookout post, a burrow in the side of a gently sloping hill.

He trained his binoculars back on the partygoers. Pretty people. Alexi had no shortage of beautiful women hanging on his arm, cavorting on his beach and soaking in his hot tub. They either didn't realize the danger surrounding the man like a miasma, or they courted it. Pretty, stupid people.

Scanning the upper-level windows again, he drew in a quick breath as a man with slicked-back white hair came into focus. He muttered, "Bingo."

Rio figured Alexi hadn't come to Maui for the sun and surf, and his CIA contact had figured the same thing. Now the proof stood at a window in Alexi's palatial rental. Alexi always used Vladimir Kolchenko, the White Russian, as the go-between for his arms deals. Kolchenko's presence in Maui guaranteed that Alexi planned to mix business with pleasure.

A bug skittered onto Rio's arm, and he flicked it off into the darkness. Now if he could just figure out a way to get into that house instead of rotting away on this spongy precipice hanging over the ocean.

A twig snapped, and he jerked to a sitting position, dropping the binoculars where they banged against his chest. He crouched by the tree growing out of the hillside to his right, his muscles tense and coiled.

Tourists, even extreme hikers, never ventured this far from the trails crisscrossing Maui's backcountry. Had Alexi's goons ferreted out his hiding place carved into the side of the hill?

His gaze tracked back and forth along the ridge of the hill, the half moon shedding a fuzzy glow on the jumble of plants that hugged the edge. A bush rustled and an object sailed over his head, dropping at his feet.

He glanced down at the crumpled flower petals littering the toes of his hiking boots.

As the foliage parted above him, a denim-clad leg appeared over the side of the ridge. The sound of a click pumped up his adrenaline, and he braced his back against the tree trunk ready to charge at the intruder.

Another leg appeared and Rio lunged forward, wrapping his arms around both appendages now dangling over the edge of the drop-off. He yanked at the legs, which kicked wildly, clamping them to his chest as he hurtled himself and his squirming package to the soft ground.

They rolled a few feet down the hillside, and although the struggling stopped, Rio received a nip on his chest through his T-shirt for his efforts. What kind of pansy-ass thugs did Prince Alexi have working for him these days? What next, hair pulling?

Their journey downhill came to a stop against a clump of bushes with Rio in the superior position, straddling the other man. Although he hadn't seen or felt a weapon during their tussle, Rio ground his knee into the intruder's right forearm while cinching his fingers around the man's narrow left wrist before he rose to a sitting position.

The branches from the trees above them obscured what little moonlight illuminated the scene. The small-statured man beneath him hadn't put up much of a fight, but Alexi's guy could be luring him into complacency.

Rio growled, "I'm going for my flashlight. If you make a move, I'll send you straight down this hill and your boss can scrape you off those rocks."

As Rio reached for his belt, he could've sworn his captive squealed. He snatched his flashlight from his belt loop, flicked it on, and shined it into the face of the limp form beneath him.

"What the hell?" He jerked back. A woman, her red hair fanning around her head, gazed at him with wide eyes. Had he just taken down an unsuspecting tourist?

He clenched his jaw and clamped his thighs tighter around her frame. Or maybe Alexi had employed a new weapon in his arsenal.

"Let me go. I don't have a boss and that includes you." She bucked beneath him, drawing up her leg to knee him in the crotch.

He dropped down onto her thighs, and she nailed him in the backside instead. "Tell me what you're doing here. How'd you find my position?"

"I'll tell you everything once you get off me. I don't know you nearly well enough for you to be straddling me like this, but buy me a couple of mai tais and you might get lucky."

She wriggled her body, and the movement, along with the exotic scent wafting from her skin, sent a shaft of desire right through to his core. Gladly, he hoisted himself up, extending a hand to her. "Get up. Don't move."

She grasped his hand, her skin smooth to the touch, and he yanked her up beside him. "Raise your arms to the side."

"You sure like tossing around the orders, don't you?"

"Just do it."

Rolling her eyes, she followed his instructions, thrusting out her arms. His flashlight trailed over her body while he patted her down with one hand. She stiffened as he passed his hand across her breasts to make sure she didn't have a weapon concealed in her bra.

When he ran his palm down her bottom and briefly

clenched her crotch, she jumped back. "Whoa. You'll have to spring for a third mai tai to get that far."

He snorted. "Don't flatter yourself, sweetheart. All you represent to me is a suspicious person in the wrong place at the wrong time."

Okay, he lied. If she did work for Mad Prince Alexi, that man possessed a brilliant strategy. This woman with her sexy body and tough talk heated his blood and stirred his passions. One helluva distraction for a stakeout.

"Satisfied I'm not packing?" Her eyes glittered in the beam of the flashlight, but he couldn't discern their color.

Satisfied? *Not at all.*

"Yeah, not much you can hide in those tight jeans and T-shirt."

She raised her brows. "Wow, you noticed my clothing?"

"I get paid to notice." He cleared his throat. "I've also noticed you're not dressed for hiking, and you don't have a backpack. So what are you doing here, and what was that click I heard right before I tackled you?"

"Click?" She scrunched up her face, but it still couldn't mar her flawless beauty. She slapped her thigh and laughed. "I found an old lighter on the ground and flicked it open and then clicked it shut. You thought that was the safety on a gun?"

He shrugged, a smile tugging at the corner of his mouth. "I guess it sounded magnified out here. That still doesn't answer my first question."

"One question at a time, cowboy." She tossed a handful of long, curly hair over one shoulder.

He scowled and shot back, "Don't call me that."

"You got something against cowboys?" She tilted her

head, and her hair tumbled over her other shoulder, its strands catching the beams from his flashlight.

His hand fisted at his side as he recalled his first and last visit to the McClintock ranch in Colorado. "Maybe. Now answer the question. The *first* question."

Folding her arms across her chest, she hunched her shoulders. "I'm out here for the same reason you are."

A muscle twitched in his jaw. What kind of game was she playing? Did some other agency have Prince Alexi under surveillance? If they did, they wouldn't send a lightweight like this woman—with no weapons and no training—no matter how gorgeous. Unless they planned to plant her inside Alexi's mansion and maybe even his bed.

His gut rolled at the thought of this woman in Alexi's clutches. Then he took a deep breath. He didn't have to rescue every scatterbrained woman on the planet.

One had been enough.

"Same reason? You mean a late-night hike?"

"Yeah, right." She kicked a gnarled root with the toe of her running shoe. "A late-night hike by yourself, huddled against the side of a hill and using mad martial arts skills to attack other tourists."

He fought against the grin stealing across his face. "Those weren't mad martial arts skills. I just yanked you off the edge of the overhang."

"Cut the crap, m-man." She covered her mouth as if stopping herself from saying more. Waving her arm behind her, she recovered. "I know why you're here, and I'm here for the same reason."

"You show me yours first, and I'll show you mine." He dug a hand in the pocket of his jeans. He had no intention of telling her his business on this hillside. But when they finished playing games here, he wouldn't mind taking her up on her invitation to buy her a mai tai…or three.

She jerked her thumb over her shoulder toward Alexi's house, now hidden by the hillside's dense foliage. "I'm here for Prince Alexi Zherkov, and so are you."

Rio widened his stance, digging the heels of his hiking boots into the mulch. The woman had her facts straight. Had the CIA hired her to work with him? If so, they hadn't bothered to tell him about it.

"Who hired you?"

She giggled, bending backward to look at the sky. "I told you…cowboy, I don't work for anyone."

"Then what's your business with Alexi?" She hardly looked like an arms dealer. Arms dealers rarely giggled.

She stopped laughing and hugged herself, her fingers biting into the taut muscles of her upper arms. For a curvy woman, she looked fit. "It's not business. It's personal."

Rio wiped the back of his hand across his brow, shoving the hair from his face. Great. Was she one of Alexi's scorned lovers? Apparently, the guy had hordes of them.

Biting the inside of his cheek, he studied the woman's face, now set in hard, determined lines. If she had a burning desire to get back at Alexi, he might be able to use her.

He doused the flare of protectiveness that leaped in his chest. It would be dangerous for her, but if she wanted revenge, they could help each other. Any woman foolish or greedy enough to hop in the sack with Mad Prince Alexi was already playing with fire. What were a few more licks from the flame?

She disappointed him. He figured a sassy woman like

her would have too much pride and self-confidence to get tangled up with a scumbag like Alexi.

"Dumped you, huh?" He smirked.

Wedging her hands on her hips, she took a step back. "You think I'm one of those bimbos, who's hanging out with a rich guy regardless of the source of those riches? You think I'm a chick who wants revenge on a player?"

"In a word—yes."

She laughed again, this time doubling over at the waist, her long hair almost touching the leaves on the ground.

No wonder Alexi had dumped her—she was insane. As nuts as Alexi was, he wouldn't have the patience for another lunatic...even one whose looks put those women in his hot tub to shame.

She unfolded her body, wiping the tears from her face. She sniffled as she wound her hair around her hand and tossed it behind her. "Oh, it's much worse than that, cowboy."

His brows shot up. This woman was throwing him more zigzags than that mountain road he'd traveled on his way up here. "Worse? Did he double-cross you in a business deal?"

"You don't listen too good for a secret agent, do you? I told you, I have a personal issue with Alexi, not a business one. I don't have anything to do with drugs, or arms or any of Alexi's other sleazy endeavors."

At least she had no misconceptions about Alexi or his business. "So what is it?"

She squared her shoulders and raised her chin. "I have the dubious distinction of being the ex-Mrs. Alexi Zherkov."

Rio's mouth dropped open. Mad Prince Alexi's mysterious former princess. In the flesh.

From his research on Alexi these past six months since the CIA had hired him to get something on the arms dealer and bring him down, Rio had learned Alexi had an ex-wife somewhere. He'd even heard that Alexi had chosen an American for his bride, but Rio's attempts to track her down and discover any more information had met with a brick wall.

Alexi kept mum about his personal life, as did those surrounding him. Rio had gotten close to only one informant, and he didn't belong to Alexi's inner circle. The mole had told Rio about an American ex-wife named Victoria. If he had known any more than that, he'd taken it to his grave after the *Landespolizei* had dragged his body out of the Rhine River near Munich.

Her bright gaze searched his face. "So you see, you can't tell me anything about that SOB down there that I don't already know. And I have as much right to be on this hillside as you do, spying on him, waiting for him to slip up so you can take him down. I don't know why you boys in the CIA think you can get him now. You've been trying for years without much luck."

He studied her pale face from beneath half-lidded eyes. She thought he was CIA. He wouldn't bother to correct her. She hit the nail on the head with one statement. The CIA had been trying for a long time to trip up Alexi. That's why the Agency hired him—to try more unconventional methods.

"So you're Victoria."

She nodded slowly, her chin dropping to her chest. "You're good, cowboy. I'm practically a state secret back in Alexi's country, good old Glazkova. What else do you know?"

"That's about it." He spread his hands wide. "Why don't you fill me in, and while you're at it, tell me why you're stalking your ex-husband."

"First off, you might as well get the name straight. I'm Tori not Victoria." She opened her arms. "Have you ever seen anyone less like a staid, proper Victoria?"

She thrust one curvy hip to the side, and Rio's eyes followed as if pulled by a magnetic force. In the muted glow of the flashlight, his gaze tracked over Tori's luscious body. A riot of red curls tumbled over one ripe breast snug in a thin T-shirt raised above her jeans and showing a strip of her flat, hard belly.

He swallowed. Nope, nothing staid or proper about her.

Leaves crackled above them and Rio froze, killing his light. A thwacking noise disturbed the silence of the hillside. Tori hissed and Rio held a finger to his lips.

A man uttered a curse in a guttural tone and another male voice answered him as the two voices floated over them in the night air.

"I don't see nothing down there."

"Tim's working lookout on the balcony, and he said he saw a light on the hillside."

Damn. He'd been careless. Rio slid the butt of the flashlight into his belt as his gaze traveled back to Tori, her hand bunched into a fist against her hip. Too many distractions.

The voices, sounding closer, continued. "That light could've been anything. Tim sent us on a wild goose chase for nothing."

"You wanna climb over the side and check it out?"

"Hell no. You wanna slide down that hillside and hit those rocks on your way into the ocean? My loyalty to Alexi only goes so far."

"I'll tell him you said that. I'm going over."

Even if Rio could find sufficient cover for himself and Tori, he couldn't allow Alexi's goons to discover his backpack with his weapon inside. He'd have to grab that, and then they'd have to…leave.

He nestled his lips close to Tori's ear and whispered, "Do what I tell you to do and just maybe I can save your life."

She drew a quick breath and jerked away from him. "How are we going to get out of here?"

He held up his hand to her, palm out, and crept toward his pack, hunching forward. As he expected, leaves and twigs crackled beneath his hiking boots. This time when Rio heard the click, he knew someone had released the safety on a real gun, not a lighter.

One of the men said, "There's something down there. I'm going to check it out."

Rio grabbed his backpack and spun around, lurching toward Tori. He gripped her arm, yanking her along a jumbled path.

She whispered, "Where are we going?"

A crack resounded behind them, and the bright beam from a powerful flashlight skimmed across their legs.

Rio rounded the corner of the makeshift trail, pulling Tori behind him. When the ocean stretched below them like smooth glass, he knew they'd reached the escape route.

Gripping Tori's hand, he pulled her to his side. He then removed his hiking boots and flung them skyward. "We're following those boots."

Her perfect lips formed an O, but before she could utter a sound, Rio pushed off from the side of the hill with his bare feet taking the former Princess of Glazkova with him into the inky blue Pacific.

Chapter Two

Tori hit the water feetfirst and tunneled into its warm embrace. When she and McClintock had made contact with the ocean, the force ripped her hand from his. She bobbed to the surface and toed off her sneakers while she twisted her head around looking for the maniac who had pulled her off a perfectly good hill into the sea.

She screamed as a dark shape emerged beside her.

"Shh." McClintock grabbed her flailing arm. "They didn't see us. There's a beach around this bend. Can you swim?"

"You're asking that question now?" Tori's legs felt like lead as she treaded water with the heavy denim of her jeans clinging to her.

"You looked like an athletic woman." He sluiced his dark hair back from the sharp planes of his face. "This way."

She paddled after the form slicing through the water, and then pulled up straight and yanked off her jeans. She didn't plan on drowning within sight of Alexi's palatial rental. That would give her ex too much satisfaction.

McClintock floated on the surface of the water and called back, "You okay?"

Free of her jeans, Tori skimmed through the calm

ocean toward him. "As long as there are no sharks out here, I'll be fine."

When she drew abreast of him, he placed his hands on her shoulders. "Sorry about that. I couldn't leave my backpack for them to find, and I knew they'd hear me when I collected it. We had to get out of there, and I'd already scoped out this escape route."

"Some escape route—a twenty-foot drop into the dark ocean." The pressure of his hands through her thin, wet T-shirt soothed her, and judging by his size and talents she figured he could take on a shark if it came to that.

"Better than facing the wrong end of a gun. Follow me."

Did she have a choice? They swam side by side, and just as Tori's muscles started burning, a strip of white sand beckoned beyond the breakwater. They headed for the shore, and got some assistance from the gentle waves cascading onto the sand.

Tori allowed the final wave to carry her in where she collapsed on the sand and gulped moist air into her lungs. McClintock crouched beside her, not even breathing heavily after their unexpected swim.

"That's it. Take a few deep breaths. I'm going to check out the contents of my backpack."

The moon, no longer hidden by the dense trees on the hill, cast a warm glow over the beach. McClintock unzipped his pack and started pulling out a few items.

While her heart hammered in her chest, Tori stretched out on the wet sand as she watched McClintock dig through his backpack. She'd almost slipped up earlier by calling him McClintock, which he was, just not the McClintock she'd expected.

As soon as she had looked up at him, straddling her body after he had yanked her from the ledge, she had realized her mistake. When her friend in the FBI, Dana McClintock, had given her the tip about Alexi's whereabouts, she'd mentioned that her husband's brother was on his trail. Tori had expected to find Ryder McClintock, a CIA operative, on the job.

But she'd grown up with sandy-haired, blue-eyed Ryder McClintock, and this man with his long, black hair and brooding dark eyes looked nothing like the Nordic McClintocks. But she'd guessed his identity immediately.

This McClintock came from the wrong side of the blanket—one of old Ralph McClintock's indiscretions. She'd heard all about how the McClintock brothers discovered the existence of an illegitimate half brother almost a year ago.

When Dana, Rafe McClintock's wife, had given her the tip about Alexi they'd both been on cell phones. All Tori heard was McClintock brother…tracking…Alexi… Maui. That's all she needed to know.

She hadn't known how to play it when faced with this gorgeous stranger instead of her childhood friend, Ryder McClintock. She knew Ryder would've helped her in true McClintock fashion. She had her doubts about this one. How much McClintock blood did he have running through his veins?

He shoved the items, including a gun, back into the pack and pushed to his feet. "Are you ready? There's a small town less than a mile ahead."

He'd shed his own jeans in the water, and his wet boxers clung to his muscular thighs. His T-shirt outlined the hard planes of his chest as water dripped from the ends of his shoulder-length dark hair.

Tilting her head back, she shifted her gaze from all

that blatant maleness on display to his face. McClintock's nostrils flared like an animal sensing his mate's desire.

Stop, Tori. She burrowed her fists into the wet sand. Her impulsiveness had always gotten her into trouble in the past, including this current mess with her ex. Time to think with her head instead of other parts of her anatomy.

She tossed a handful of sand into the air. "Uh, we're both a little underdressed to be walking the streets of a small town."

"We're in Maui." He shrugged his broad shoulders. "The clothes we have on look like beach casual around here but if you'd like to wear my T-shirt into town, it'll cover you up pretty thoroughly."

He grabbed the hem of his shirt and started to roll it up, revealing a set of ripped abs.

Jumping to her feet, Tori stopped him. "That's okay. If you lose your shirt, you'll be half-naked. Don't want to call too much attention to ourselves."

And she couldn't be held accountable for her actions if she had to traipse along the beach next to a wet Adonis.

She tugged at her own T-shirt molded to her body, pulling it over her underwear. "Okay, then what do we do in town?"

He pointed to the lights up the coast as he took a long step forward. "I left my car there before hiking into the hills. Where's your car? And how did you happen to stumble on my lookout?"

While she sawed her bottom lip, Tori trudged after him, her feet slapping against the hard sand. She usually handled a defense with a good offense.

"What's your name anyway? You know mine."

He spun around and extended his hand while walking backward. "McClintock. Rio McClintock."

She grabbed his hand, and the sand on his palm chafing her own still couldn't block that electric current she felt every time her skin met his.

So the illegitimate brother rated one of the McClintock R names. Ralph had named his boys Rod, Ryder and Rafe. How had the black sheep ended up with one of those? Although Rio had a different ring to it, kind of exotic and definitely sexy.

He yanked her toward him and she stumbled. "Sorry." He steadied her with a firm hand placed on her hip. "Now how did you know I was out there, or did you?"

Two of his fingers rested on the bare flesh between the bottom of her skimpy T-shirt and her bikini undies. That one bit of contact set her skin on fire. She swiveled away from him. She had to keep her wits about her if she didn't want to reveal too much too soon.

"I have a contact on the inside. I knew…someone was on my ex-husband's trail here in Maui. I watched the waters in front of Alexi's compound but didn't notice anyone out there. The hillside caught my attention as the best place to spy on the activities in that house, so I headed out for a hike. I didn't know you were on the other side of the hill until you pulled me over."

"I'm impressed. That's a helluva hike, especially without any gear or even a flashlight."

"Save your admiration. I came with one of those hiking tour groups, told the guide I was meeting a friend for the hike back and ditched them. They supplied all the accoutrements, which I left on the bus. I didn't figure it would get so dark so fast out here and didn't even think about a flashlight."

Rio rolled his eyes, and a sharp pain stabbed her gut.

He'd already pegged her as an idiot—flighty, impulsive—the same qualities Prince Alexi had seen in her and used to his advantage.

"Not so impressive, huh?" She glanced down, burrowing her toes into the wet sand.

"I wouldn't say that. You still made it to the edge of that ridge in the dark without killing yourself. You must lead a charmed life." He turned away from the water, heading toward the twinkling lights.

"Yeah, supercharmed," she said to his broad back.

They scuffed through the dry sand in silence until they reached a paved path bordering the beach.

Rio swung the backpack off his shoulder. "I have some money with me. I'm sure there are a few tourist shops still open where we can get some dry clothes."

Tori pinched the material of her damp T-shirt between two fingers and let it snap back. "Mine's almost dry. I could use some shorts though."

"And I'm guessing a ride back to…wherever you're staying."

"One of the hotels on Kaanapali Beach. You know, blend in with the rest of the tourists." She didn't mention she had plans to relocate to Alexi's ostentatious complex overlooking the ocean. She just had a few loose ends to tie up before the move. And Rio McClintock represented one, big loose end.

Her gaze wandered to Rio's tight buttocks outlined by the edge of his T-shirt, and she smirked. *Okay, not exactly a loose end.*

"I'm glad you find our situation funny. You've completely torpedoed that hiding place for me. Even if Alexi's thugs never realized they chased a couple of people off that hillside instead of a couple of animals, they'll be watching that location now."

The fact that Rio wouldn't have that secret lookout gave a big boost to her scheme. "Don't blame me. You're the one who yanked me off the edge of the hill and tackled me. Otherwise, I wouldn't have even known you were burrowed in your little hole."

They emerged onto the main street of the small town. Lights glowed from the shops up and down the street, open for business for people returning from nighttime hikes or a visit to the volcano. The Christmas decorations looked incongruous against the backdrop of swaying palm trees and the smell of suntan lotion.

She had no intention of spending Christmas in Maui.

Rio pulled her back from the street, tucking her behind his solid back. "Hold on. Let me check things out first."

"Suspicious, aren't you?"

He glanced over his shoulder. "That's a quality you should've exercised before you got married."

"Touché." He got that right, although he didn't have to rub it in. If she'd been more leery of and less flattered by Alexi's attentions and frantic pursuit of her, she wouldn't be in this mess.

"Okay, coast is clear." He grabbed her hand and made a beeline for the nearest clothing store.

"What's the worry?"

"Those two guys on the hillside had to have left their car here. I don't want to run into them. Who knows? Maybe they know you. You don't want your ex to find out you're here, do you?"

Not yet anyway and not in the company of a CIA agent.

"You're right. Alexi had a lot of loyal minions." Minions who'd spied on her and kept her a prisoner in her own home in Glazkova. "Some of the ones I knew might still be working for him. It's kind of a lifetime employment gig. If you leave, you have to retire…permanently."

"I know you're joking, but you're not too far from the truth. Anyone who has any information about Alexi's business is a danger to him."

"Who said I was joking?" She pushed past him and entered the shop.

The young woman reading a magazine at the counter looked up when they walked through the door. Her eyes widened as she took in their underwear. "Looks like you guys need some clothes right now."

Rio shrugged and grinned. "We went skinny-dipping and the waves carried our clothes out to sea. We recovered everything but our pants."

The clerk's gaze meandered over Rio's half-naked body and the corner of her mouth lifted in a smile. "That's one of the dangers of skinny-dipping. You have to make sure you leave your stuff on the dry sand."

"We were kind of in a hurry." Rio curled his arm around Tori's waist, pulling her in for a hug, hip to hip.

Tori nestled close to his body, resting a hand on his buttocks, the muscles under the thin material of his boxers firm beneath her fingertips. He went there first. She may as well contribute to the reality of the lie.

"Yeah, I hear ya." The clerk scooted around the counter and as she brushed past Tori, she whispered, "Lucky girl."

Tori wished she and Rio had been skinny-dipping instead of escaping from Alexi's thugs in the open ocean after a twenty-foot drop. She'd left those carefree days behind her a lifetime ago.

The woman gestured to a rack of men's shorts and board shorts, and then pointed to a wall of women's shorts. "We have a lot of new styles. The dressing rooms are in the corner."

After they both picked out some shorts and wore them out of the dressing rooms, Rio paid at the counter with slightly damp bills and they left the store.

Tori had to admit the man still looked delicious even with a pair of baggy shorts hanging almost to his knees. He must work undercover for the CIA because he wasn't as clean-cut as his half brother, Ryder McClintock, who also worked for the CIA. Strange coincidence that two half brothers, who didn't know each other and didn't grow up together, both landed with the CIA. Must be that protective instinct they shared.

An instinct Tori intended to exploit.

"Before I take you back to your hotel, do you want a shaved ice?" He pointed to a little shop on the corner. "Best shaved ice in Maui."

Tori figured he'd decided to sweeten her up. Pump her for information about Alexi. She had plenty to share, but she planned to do it her way and on her terms.

"Sounds great. I am so thirsty."

He dug into his backpack and waved a bottle of water in her face. "You should've asked. If you don't mind sharing germs."

She snatched the bottle from his hand and chugged the rest of the water. Hell, she didn't mind sharing germs with this guy.

They ordered a couple of shaved ices and settled on the bench outside the store to watch a handful of people wandering in and out of the shops on the street.

"So how did you meet Prince Alexi of Glazkova?"

That didn't take long. "I was vacationing in Glazkova, and I met him at a private party at one of the casinos."

"You must run with the pretty people. Not every

tourist vacationing in Glazkova rates an invitation to a private party with the Prince in attendance."

"I had a lot of friends in the international party set." Tori shoveled a spoonful of ice drenched in sweet syrup into her mouth to get rid of the sour taste as she remembered those days of languid pleasure in Glazkova.

"How long were you married?" Rio jabbed his spoon into the dome of red ice, scattering ice chips onto the pavement.

"Two years, two months, and twelve days. Or at least that's how long we stayed together. The actual divorce came a little later."

He raised an eyebrow. "How many hours?"

"Umm, about nine." She slurped some grape-flavored ice onto her tongue.

"Did the excitement wear off or just the opposite? Did the fun and games get too hot to handle?"

"You're right. This shaved ice is the best." He must've been smoking some Maui wowi on that hillside if he thought she'd cough up the dirt on Alexi for nothing in return. Besides, she had only old dirt on Alexi. If he wanted fresh dirt he'd have to pay.

He laughed. "You're sharp, Princess Tori."

"That's ex-Princess Tori to you, McClintock. I can't tell you anything about Alexi's current operation, so you might as well find another lookout post."

He gripped her wrist so suddenly, she dropped her spoon.

"Then what *are* you doing here? Do you miss the high life? Are you making a ploy to get back into Alexi's bed? Because let me tell you, sweetheart, you have plenty of competition. He has scads of scantily clad beautiful women roaming all over that compound."

She snorted. "Is that why you're keeping such a close watch on his house?"

She tried to jerk away from him, but the strong fingers cinched tighter around her wrist. "Cut the crap, Tori. Why are you here? What kind of revenge do you want on Alexi?"

Flexing her fingers, she watched a couple and their two children emerge from the T-shirt shop across the street. Time to 'fess up. She didn't want Rio to think she was stalking Alexi so she could jump in the sack with him. That notion seemed to really bother him.

Two men rounded the corner. Rio had loosened his grip on her wrist, but now it tightened. Still talking, the men got into a black Hummer parked at the curb.

Rio tossed his cup into the trashcan next to the bench and pulled Tori to her feet. He dragged her into the doorway of a souvenir shop, closed for the night.

The Hummer's engine roared to life and Rio placed a hand on her shoulder and spun her around. Weaving one hand through her hair, he pulled her close and planted a hard kiss on her mouth. As the big car rolled past them in the street, Rio shifted his body against hers, as if to protect her from the occupants of the car, and deepened the kiss.

Her heart, which had started pounding at the appearance of the two men, now raced. She clung to Rio's shoulders to keep from sliding to the ground, and he hitched an arm around her waist as if he knew she needed his support.

As the sound of the car's engine died out, Tori sagged against Rio's body, his hard muscles still primed for action. He relinquished her lips and released the hand cupping the back of her head, but stroked his fingers through her tangled curls.

Closing her eyes, she rested her forehead against his chest.

He kissed the top of her head and mumbled hoarsely, "I don't think they saw you. Probably thought we were another honeymooning couple."

She leaned back in his arms, looking into his face. Deep lines creased his handsome features. Oh, yeah. The protective streak that ran through the McClintock men hadn't bypassed Rio.

"Did you recognize them? We didn't see their faces on the hillside."

"Don't forget, I've been watching the compound for weeks. I've seen those two patrolling the grounds."

"D-do you think they were looking for us?" Despite her determination to face Alexi and bring him down, she shivered. She hadn't been able to let go in a long time, but here in this man's arms she allowed herself to crumble just a little.

Rio ran a hand down her back. "I don't think they know what they're looking for, probably not a couple kissing on the sidewalk."

"Quick thinking, McClintock." Her lips ached to feel the pressure of his sweet, cherry-flavored kiss again, but they didn't have any more excuses to engage in another lip-lock.

Tugging her out of their cozy alcove, he said, "Let's get you back to your hotel, and then you're checking out and getting on the first flight back to...wherever it is you came from."

She didn't figure Rio would send her packing before he tried to interrogate her further about Alexi's business deals, habits and friends. She planted her bare feet on the sidewalk. "Oh, no you don't. I'm not leaving until I get what I came here for."

"If the guy divorced you, he's not going to be too happy to see you again, especially if he figures out you have revenge on your mind. An unhappy Mad Prince Alexi is a dangerous Mad Prince Alexi. You of all people should know that."

"I do know that, but it doesn't change a thing. I have to carry out my plan."

Rio stuffed his hands in the pockets of his new shorts. "What exactly is your plan?"

Tori scooped in a deep breath. "I'm moving into Alexi's compound."

"Are you crazy?" Rio's fists bulged in his pockets. "What makes you think he'll let you in there?"

Lifting her chin, she squared her shoulders. "Oh, he'll let me in."

"Then what? You're going to try some revenge scheme? You'll be putting yourself in extreme danger. It's worse than it was two years ago. Back then he was moving drugs and dabbling in arms. Now he's a full-scale arms dealer, working with the most lethal terrorist groups in the world."

"That's why it's more vital than ever that I move into the compound."

He grabbed her shoulders and shook her. "Why? Why is it so important for you to do this?"

She caught her bottom lip between her teeth as tears flooded her eyes. "My son's in there."

Chapter Three

Tori's words twisted a knife in his gut, and his grip on her shoulders melted into a caress. As her bottom lip trembled, he pulled her back into his arms, where she'd felt so right before.

His contact hadn't told him about a child, and Rio hadn't seen any evidence of one at the compound, although he hadn't been able to spy on the south wing as it lay on the other side of the property. All of the guests and the parties congregated in the rooms and terraces on the north and northwest ends of the compound, which placed them right in his line of fire.

Even a poor excuse for a father like Alexi would want to keep his son away from that crowd.

Tori sniffled against his chest and Rio stroked her wild curls. How had a woman like this, bright and feisty as all hell, gotten mixed up with a lunatic like Prince Alexi?

And what idiot at the CIA had told Alexi's ex-wife about the operation against him?

Tori stepped back, wiping the back of her hand across her cheek. "That's why I have to get into that compound. I haven't been allowed to see my boy in almost two years."

From what he knew about Alexi, that didn't surprise

Rio. An arrogant, possessive man like Alexi wouldn't readily relinquish custody of his son.

"What makes you think he's going to let you see him now?"

Lifting her shoulders, she said, "He's in the U.S. now. I could cause some legal trouble for him if he tries to keep me away from Max. Alexi doesn't like attention like that."

The lights up and down the street began to blink off as the shops closed for business. Rio laced his fingers through Tori's. "Let's finish this discussion in my car."

Rio had parked his rental on a side street behind a truck. After he tossed his backpack into the trunk and settled behind the wheel, he turned to Tori.

"Where has your son been all this time—Glazkova?"

She nodded. "And if you think the security is tight at his spread here in Maui, you should see it at his palace in Glazkova."

"Can't you visit your son there?" Rio cranked on the engine and pulled onto the darkened main street. He figured the Hummer would be heading back to Alexi's property, and Tori's hotel lay in the other direction.

Rolling down her window, Tori snorted. "I'm persona non grata in Glazkova. I'm not even allowed to step foot in the country or I'll get tossed into prison. There's a warrant for my arrest."

Rio's brows shot up. "For what?"

"Adultery."

"What?"

"Adultery is a crime punishable by at least two years of hard labor in a lovely Glazkova prison, but of course it was a trumped-up charge. Even if I'd wanted to cheat on Alexi, he made sure I'd never have an opportunity to do so."

Rio's jaw tightened at the hardships this woman had endured at the hands of that criminal. "Why did he put you through all that?"

"Because I wanted a divorce. I wanted to take my son, Max, and go home." She rubbed her hands together as if a sudden chill had grabbed her on this sultry, tropical night.

"So he accused you of adultery? Don't the Glazkova courts require some proof, or are they wholly under Prince Alexi's command?"

"They are, but even so the courts have to at least pretend there's justice for all, so Alexi made sure they had proof. He paid off or coerced members of his staff to come forward and admit they'd slept with me. By the time Alexi was through with me, everyone thought I'd serviced the entire security force of Glazkova."

Rio slanted a glance at Tori, her eyes bright with tears. He'd despised Prince Alexi for spreading misery around the world through drugs and weapons. Now he wanted to kill the man.

"So he drove you out of Glazkova and kept Max there."

"Yeah." She rubbed her nose. "I had three choices. I could go to a labor camp for two years or more, and probably not be allowed to see Max after. I could stay married to Alexi and live as a prisoner in my own home. Or I could flee the country and leave my son behind."

Her voice broke, and she buried her face in her hands. "I'm a terrible mother. I abandoned my son to save myself. I should've never left him behind."

Rio ran his hand across her heaving shoulders. "You had to save yourself. You'd be no use to your son otherwise. Given the chance, Alexi will raise that boy in his image."

Raising her head, Tori curled her hands into fists. "I know. That's why I need to get Max out of there and away from his father. Once I learned Alexi was in Hawaii and had Max with him, I saw my best chance in two years."

"How did you know he had Max with him?" The Agency hadn't even known Prince Alexi had a son, or if they did nobody had told Rio.

"I have a contact on the inside."

Rio's pulse ticked up several notches. Tori had a contact inside Alexi's compound? He hadn't been able to manage that since the last mole wound up dead. He could use an insider about now. Maybe Tori would share her guy with him.

"Who is it? One of the security guys you supposedly slept with?"

"No, a woman. Max's nanny."

Rio gripped the steering wheel. *So much for that idea.* He refused to put a woman in danger in his quest to bring down Alexi. "She's taking a huge risk helping you."

Tori shrugged. "She's a mom."

Rio rounded the curve into Lahaina and asked Tori for the name of her hotel. She gave him the name of one of the most luxurious resorts in Maui. Alexi must've paid her some big bucks in the divorce settlement, but he didn't want to judge her. Whatever monetary compensation she'd gotten out of the deal couldn't make up for what she'd lost.

Getting out of Glazkova when she did probably saved her life. When things turned sour between arms and drug dealers, the injured party usually went after his enemy… and his enemy's family. Rio had seen a few families pay the ultimate price.

The presence of Tori's son in that household filled Rio

with a cold dread and put a serious crimp in his options for bringing down Alexi. He couldn't tip off Alexi's enemies about his whereabouts and habits with a child in the house. These gangs were vicious and indiscriminate in their retaliation.

Rio rolled in front of the hotel and waved off the valet. "I'll just be a few minutes."

He cut the engine. "So how do you plan to get your son away from Alexi? Have you hired a good attorney yet?"

Tori laughed. "That's just the sort of thing that would prompt Alexi to send Max back to Glazkova, and it wouldn't work anyway. I'm going to use that as leverage though, promising Alexi that I won't bring in the U.S. legal system if he allows me to stay at the estate and see Max."

"Will just seeing Max be enough for you?" One glance at Tori's tight jaw and narrowed eyes told him it wouldn't.

"Of course not. That's just my foot in the door."

"Then what?" Rio's heart pounded against his chest like a hammer as he held his breath.

"I'm going to rescue him…and you're going to help me."

"No." RIO POUNDED the steering wheel with the heel of his hand. "I am not putting you or your child in danger with some crazy rescue plan."

Maybe she dropped this particular bombshell too soon, but Rio had to know sometime she intended to enlist his help. He'd come around once she explained the entire plan to him.

She could usually get people, especially men, to

come around. Of course, she had made that mistake with Alexi.

She ran her hands through her tangled curls. "Just wait. There's something in it for you, too."

"Do you think that's going to change my mind? I'm here to collect information about Alexi for the CIA, not to stage a rescue operation."

Drawing her brows together, she asked, "Aren't you CIA?"

He dragged in a ragged breath and blew it out, staring straight ahead. "No. A couple of my buddies from the Marines and I set up our own shop, but the Agency uses us a lot—for activities under the radar, not sanctioned by the U.S. Government."

"That's even better." She clapped her hands. The U.S. Government hadn't been much use in her quest to get Max. "D-do you ever assassinate people?"

Rio's eyes widened and his jaw dropped. "You want me to execute your ex-husband? We're not hired assassins. I'm here to turn over contacts, spy on meetings, secure a mole…."

Her heart skipped a few beats and she waved her hand. "I can be your mole."

With the veins popping out on his neck and his white-knuckled hands still grasping the steering wheel, Rio looked ready to explode.

But his words pelted the space between them in a measured staccato. "That. Can't. Happen."

"Sure it can." She patted the tensed muscles in his thigh. "I'll approach Alexi and ask him if I can move into the compound to visit Max while he's here. He'll let me because I'll promise not to cause any trouble for him with the authorities in the U.S."

With a muscle ticking in his jaw, Rio dropped his gaze

to her hand. She snatched it away and continued. "Once I'm in, I'll keep my eyes and ears open and I can feed information to you. All you need to do in exchange for my services is get Max out of that den of iniquity."

"Not only is that a dangerous proposition," he said as he loosened his grasp on the steering wheel and wiped his palms across his T-shirt, "but it'll blow my operation sky high."

"How do you figure?" Tori thought she could convince Rio by playing on his obvious sympathy for her situation and his naturally protective instincts, which he'd demonstrated in spades tonight. She didn't count on those protective instincts combining with a hardheaded stubbornness that refused to see the logic of putting herself in harm's way for a greater good.

"If I attempt some sort of rescue and meet with failure, Alexi's going to realize he's being watched, not to mention, place you in a world of hurt."

She flicked her fingers. "Alexi always thinks he's being watched anyway. And I have confidence that you won't fail."

Leaning toward him, she trailed her fingertips along his corded forearm as the ends of her hair danced on his shoulder. Rio sucked in a sharp breath, and Tori jerked back.

His dark eyes smoldered as he looked at her, and it wasn't due to lust as it had been on the beach. "You're playing me, Tori whateveryourlastnameis. How do I know any of this is true? How do I know if there's even a child at risk? I've never seen him. Maybe you did sleep with half of Alexi's security force, he banished you from a life of leisure, and now you want to use me to get revenge."

As his accusations rained down on her, the blood

rushed through her veins hot and furious. Blinded by her anger, she raised her hand to smack his face, but he caught her wrist and they glared at each other over their hands.

Tori twisted free and staggered from the car. Before she slammed the door, she choked out, "You're a sorry excuse for a McClintock."

She stormed toward the open lobby and tripped across the tiled floors toward the pool and the beach beyond. The smell of the food from a luau, now wrapping up on a lawn bordering the sand, made her stomach grumble, reminding her she hadn't eaten since the lunch provided on the hiking trip and that shaved ice.

Her bare feet hit the beach, each step digging a hole into the dry sand as she drove her heel into it, muttering epithets. Tears stung her eyes, blurring the lights from the boats scattered on the water.

How dare Rio accuse her of manipulating him?

As she reached the hard-packed sand, she slowed her steps and folded her arms across her stomach. Even though that's exactly what she'd planned to do.

She'd expected to run into Ryder watching her ex-husband and twist him around her finger, playing on his Sir Galahad complex. When confronted with Rio, she had made a smooth transition practicing her wiles on him instead.

Apparently, Rio didn't suffer from the same complex…or he had a supercharged overdose of it. He didn't even want her to place herself in danger in the first place. But then he had accused her of lying…of lying about Max.

She sank to the beach and grabbed fistfuls of sand. Max was so close she could feel the strong maternal pull toward him like a tide out to sea. She'd get into that compound to see her little boy even if she never made it out again.

The separation from her son had bored a deep, black hole in the pit of her belly. She couldn't live without him anymore.

Jumping to her feet, she chucked the sand she'd gathered into the ocean. She'd approach Alexi tomorrow, or at least his guards at the estate. Once she had Max in her arms, she'd figure out something—with or without the help of Rio McClintock.

She sauntered along the beach, dragging her feet through the white water, skirting romantic couples locked in embraces or holding hands as they strolled past her.

She swallowed around a lump in her throat. She missed having that closeness with someone, not that she'd ever really had it with Alexi. And for the past two years she'd been too busy jaunting around the world, arguing with State Department officials and consulting with lawyers, to think about romance. Besides, she had no intention of dragging some poor man into Alexi's radar. She needed a strong man for that job.

She needed…McClintock.

As her feet left the grittiness of the beach for the soft grass of the lawn that led to the path to her hotel suite, she stopped and cursed. Her room key card was out in the ocean somewhere securely in the pocket of her jeans.

She veered back toward the pool where several guests still frolicked in the warm night air. Approaching the front desk, she smiled. "I lost my room key on a hike today. I'm in fifty-one twenty-five."

The desk clerk requested her name and then tilted her

head as she punched some keys on the computer keyboard. "Someone left a package for you, Ms. Scott."

"A package?" Tori squeaked the words out past her tight throat. She hadn't told anyone about her plans, except Dana.

The clerk dipped below the front desk and placed a bulky manila envelope on the counter. Tori ran her fingers along the edges. "Who left this?"

"I'm sorry. I don't know. I came on duty five minutes ago, so it wasn't in the past five minutes. And I can't tell when the previous clerk entered the note on the computer." She slid two white cards next to the package. "I'm giving you an extra key card, Ms. Scott."

Tori nodded and swept the cards and the package from the counter. She sank onto a wicker sofa in the lobby and ripped into the envelope. Flower petals showered onto her lap, their cloying scent making her gag on her empty stomach.

She dumped the lei onto the cushion next to her and fingered the dead, rotting flowers. This lei didn't mean aloha and welcome. Had Alexi sent this? He'd always favored dramatic gestures.

Sighing, she struggled to her feet and dumped the envelope into the nearest trash can. Oh, well, it's not like she wanted to continue skulking around the island hoping to get a glimpse of her son. She'd leave the skulking to Rio.

Tori wound her way back to the path that led to a bank of elevators beyond the pool. A few couples, returning from late dinners, crisscrossed the hallways and expansive floors, open to the outside. But when Tori reached her floor, silence greeted her.

She hadn't seen the other inhabitants of this floor

since she got here. They probably chose this out-of-the-way wing for privacy.

Same reason she chose it.

She slid the new key card into the slot and waited for the green light to flash. She frowned. Not even a red light flashed. She tried again and got the same response—nothing.

She switched cards and tried the second one. Again, nothing.

Grinding her teeth, she kicked the door. The desk clerk had given her the wrong key cards, and now she had to haul her butt all the way back to the lobby. And she wanted nothing more than to peel off her disgusting clothes, hop in the shower, and down a little twenty dollar bottle of wine from the minibar.

In frustration, she grabbed the doorknob. It not only turned, but the door inched open. She guessed the key card worked after all, but the lights must be broken.

She leaned her hip against the heavy door and pushed. Before she could flick on the hall light, something came at her out of the darkness.

A scream barreled up from her lungs. A rough hand clapped over her mouth while a heavy arm wrapped around her stomach.

She struggled, pounding her heel against a bare shin, but the vice clamped tighter around her midsection. She gagged as garlic-scented breath whispered against her ear.

"Do you want to die, Princess?"

Chapter Four

Rio clenched the steering wheel as he hit the highway back to his little bungalow. That's not how he'd planned to end the evening with the Princess of Glazkova.

He had no intention of allowing her to jump into her ex-husband's snake pit, but he could've coaxed some information from her about her son's nanny. The nanny could lead to other chinks in the Zherkov armor. Maybe pinpoint a disgruntled employee, someone willing to turn on Alexi for immunity and a chance to escape a life of crime.

Time to make nice.

He wheeled his car into the next turnout and made a U-turn back to Tori. And just to make sure his return trip meant business and not pleasure, he clicked open the glove compartment to grab his cell phone. Good thing he hadn't taken his cell with him on the surveillance or he'd be looking for a new phone.

His CIA contact, Ted Boyce, picked up on the first ring. Must've been waiting for him. "Ted, I have some interesting news."

"Hope so because the Agency is wondering if you took this gig to get an all-expenses-paid trip to Maui."

Rio snorted. "Yeah, I've been having such a relaxing

time. You can tell your buddies that I ran into Zherkov's ex-wife."

Ted drew in a breath. "Ding, ding, ding. You hit the jackpot, bro. What's she doing there and how'd you manage to hook up with her?"

Not so fast. Rio wasn't ready to give up all of Tori's secrets. He didn't want the Agency jumping the gun on anything. He could still out-CIA the CIA. He cleared his throat. "She's here because he's here."

"Can we use her?"

The edges of his phone bit into Rio's flesh as he gripped it. That's exactly why he didn't want the CIA to get its grubby paws on Tori. "I'll keep you posted."

His lips twisted as he slid his phone shut. *Way to keep it professional, McClintock.*

Rio pulled up in front of the hotel and slid from the car. The valet parking attendant scurried toward him, holding out a ticket between outstretched fingers. "Are you a guest at the hotel, sir?"

"No. Does that mean I can't leave my car here?"

A smile flickered across the younger man's face. "You can leave it here, but it costs more."

"Of course it does." Rio snatched the ticket from the valet's hand and stalked toward the registration desk.

People with leis draped around their necks milled about the lobby. The sweet, heavy scent from the plumeria conjured images of lazy nights on the beach with a fruity cocktail in one hand and a sultry woman in the other.

Rio shook his head. That twenty-foot jump into the ocean must've fogged his brain…or maybe his companion on that jump had something to do with his line of thinking.

The desk clerk smiled as he approached. He didn't

play the part of friendly tourist very well, but he pasted on his best gee-whiz grin. "I'm meeting a friend here. Could you please tell me her room number?"

With her smile still in place, the woman shook her head. "I'm sorry. We can't give out our guest's room numbers. If you give me your friend's name, I can call the room."

Damn. No way Tori would be using Zherkov for her last name. Rio chuckled and rolled his eyes. "To tell you the truth—" he peered at her badge "—Marissa, I met the young lady at a bar earlier tonight. Didn't catch her last name."

She pursed her lips and raised her brows. "I suppose I can do a search on her first name, as long as it's not too common."

"Tori." Rio let out a long breath. "She's staying in a suite if that helps."

"It does." The clerk clicked some keys on her keyboard and picked up the phone. She listened for several seconds and then shrugged. "Your friend isn't in her room, or at least she's not picking up."

A trill of alarm rushed up Rio's spine. He abandoned the horny tourist act and reached into his backpack for his wallet. He smacked a CIA ID badge on the counter and narrowed his eyes. "Ma'am, it's vitally important that I get that room number…now."

With eyes wide, she scanned the badge and his picture. Then she drew back and fumbled for a piece of paper. Nice and polite never did work for him, but forceful and threatening always did the job.

"You don't need to write it down. Just tell me the number."

It took her two tries to babble out, "Fifty-one twenty-five. Take the elevators past the pool and across from the spa."

He slung his backpack over one shoulder and jogged across the pool deck. Damp grass squished between his toes as he made his way to the darkened spa and the bank of elevators.

Maybe Tori didn't answer her phone because she was afraid it might be Alexi. But if she wanted access to his compound, she'd have to talk to her ex sometime. She could be in the shower.

Rio punched the elevator button with his fist until the doors whisked open. On his way into the car, he bumped shoulders with an intoxicated man stumbling from the elevator. The man grabbed his date's arm and scowled at Rio.

"Watch whereya goin'."

Rio skewered the drunk with a lethal gaze, and he tripped against the woman. She tugged his arm. "Let's go, Adam."

The doors closed on the couple, and Rio's muscles tensed as he rode up the five floors to Tori's suite. The elevator deposited him on an open floor facing the beach and the ocean. He crossed the tiles toward an alcove that looked like it contained two rooms.

As he drew near to fifty-one twenty-five, a low voice rumbled from the door, which was ajar. A woman's voice responded, high-pitched, frantic.

Adrenaline pumped through Rio's body and he charged the door, kicking it open. The door hit a body, and a large man broke away from Tori, his hands dropping from her throat. Rio bared his teeth and drew back his fist.

"Stop." Tori grabbed his forearm.

Rio glanced down into her green eyes and she had

the temerity to scowl at him. Hadn't he just saved her life? Twice now? Or was it three times? He dropped his fist.

"It's okay. I know this man." Tori stepped behind Rio. "And he was just leaving."

Tori's attacker grunted as he eyed Rio's still-clenched hand. "Who's this guy?"

"I don't know. A guest at the hotel, I suppose. Are you staying on this floor?"

Rio bent a kink out of his neck and flexed his fingers. He almost blew his cover in front of one of Alexi's men. He scanned the burly man from his greasy hair to his dirty running shoes. Definitely one of Alexi's goons.

"Yeah, I just came up to get my wife a sweater when I heard the commotion in here. Are you sure you're okay?"

"I'm okay." Tori straightened her spine. "Just a little disagreement."

The man's face split into a grin, displaying rows of bad teeth. "A disagreement."

Rio shrugged and backed away to the door across the alcove, delving into the pocket of his shorts, pretending to search for his key card.

"You'll pass along my message?"

"Sure, but don't get your hopes up." The man turned and ambled toward the elevator while Tori shut her hotel room door.

Rio watched from the corner of his eye until Alexi's man disappeared into the elevator, and then he spun around and banged on Tori's door.

Her muffled voice came from behind the door. "Who is it?"

"It's me."

She flung open the door, her brows drawn over her

nose. "You almost stepped in it, cowboy. If Alexi's thug reported back to my ex that I was in town with a body-guard in tow, I'd never get near that compound. Not to mention your own gig would blow up in your face."

"You're welcome, princess." He brushed past her into the spacious suite and dropped his backpack on the coffee table. "The next time you're getting manhandled by a giant with greasy hair and an acne-scarred face, I'll keep on walking."

Tori's shoulders slumped as she closed the door and locked it. "Thanks. I'm glad you came to the rescue even though you could've screwed up my plans. That guy scared the crap out of me."

"What did he want and how'd your ex know you were in Maui?"

"One of his guys saw me in Lahaina and tracked me back to this hotel. Not that I was trying to hide from Alexi, and I explained that to my uninvited guest."

Rio sucked in a breath. "Has Alexi been tailing you?"

"No. Believe me, the hike left early enough this morn-ing that I would've noticed if someone were following me."

"So did you get a chance to tell Alexi's guy that you're in Maui to see your son?"

She nodded, running fingers through her tangled curls. "I tried to assure him I didn't want any trouble but told him I needed to speak to Alexi."

"But you are looking for trouble."

Tori crossed her arms and leaned a shoulder against the door. "What are you doing here?"

"I came to apologize." Rio bent forward and opened the door to the mini bar. No beer, just little bottles of wine that he could finish off in a few gulps.

"Really?" She pushed off the door and joined him at

the minibar. She reached over his shoulder, her hair a whisper against the back of his neck. She snagged two bottles of chardonnay from the fridge and waved one in his face. "Want one?"

"Sure, but don't look so cheerful. I'm still not agreeing to your plan."

She tossed back her hair and twisted open her bottle with a crack. A red mark marred her creamy skin, and Rio traced his finger along her jaw.

"Did he do that?"

Tori shivered. "He got kind of carried away when he slapped his hand over my mouth to stop my scream."

Scumbag. Rio's fingers wrapped around the sweating bottle so tightly, it almost slipped from his grasp. He cupped Tori's face with his other hand.

"Are you all right? Do you want some ice?" He held up the wine. "A cold bottle?"

"A drink will do me." She put her lips to the bottle and took a swig, but her hand shook and she swayed on her feet.

Rio set his wine bottle on top of the minibar, placed Tori's next to it and rested his hands on her shoulders. The cotton of her T-shirt, stiff with salt water and sand, stuck to the rough pads of his fingertips. "You need a warm shower and probably something to eat, right?"

"Those were my plans before tall, dark and ugly busted in here." She pulled her trembling bottom lip between her teeth, squaring her shoulders beneath his touch.

Rio almost pulled her into his arms to comfort, to protect, but her glittering green eyes warned him to back off. This woman would fight the devil himself to stay on her feet and keep trudging onward. Working on her own obviously came naturally to her. She'd probably already exhausted every legal channel to get her son back from Prince Alexi.

Now she'd decided to look into a few illegal channels.

If she wouldn't accept a shoulder to cry on, Rio could at least offer her something more practical. He spun her around and gave her a shove toward the cavernous bathroom. "Go take a shower and I'll order from room service. Anything you won't eat?"

"Crow."

Rolling his eyes, Rio grabbed her wine bottle and one of the glasses on the credenza. He dumped the contents of the bottle into the glass and handed it to her. "Nobody's going to force you to eat crow."

The door snapped behind her and Rio picked up the phone and punched in the extension for room service. He ordered a couple of cheeseburgers and fries. No crow.

While Tori cranked on the shower, Rio wandered around the spacious sitting room. Tori must've gotten a lot of money in the divorce, but he figured she'd trade it all to get her son back.

He'd seen this type of predicament before—American woman marries a foreigner, lives in his country, has his children. And then when the marriage goes south, the wife can't leave the country with her children.

The fact that Tori married royalty and royalty-gone-bad made her situation much worse. What had she been thinking when she said *I do* to Mad Prince Alexi?

Rio pulled back the drapes and slid open the door to the balcony. The soft, warm breeze whispered against his skin, carrying with it a whiff of some sweet flower and a salty tang from the ocean that he could taste on his tongue. He sipped his wine and soaked up the scenery.

"Nice view, huh?"

Rio shifted his gaze from the dark ocean where lights from a few dinner cruises and other pleasure craft bobbed and blinked to the glass sliding door and Tori's reflection. She clutched a white robe around her body and had wrapped up her hair in a towel that made her look like the Chiquita banana lady.

He turned and propped his shoulder blade against the doorjamb. "Feel better?"

"I do. You should try it."

Rio shrugged off the door. "I wasn't the one manhandled by Alexi's thug. I ordered some cheeseburgers. Is that okay?"

"Sounds great." She patted the knot in the sash across her stomach.

"Can I ask you a few questions about Alexi?"

Tori bent over at the waist, rubbed her head with the towel and then flipped her head up, her wet hair already spiraling into curls. "What do I get out of it?"

"If I can bring in Alexi and turn him over to the CIA, you'll get your son back."

"Ha!" She tossed the wet towel into the bathroom and shoved her hands into the pockets of the hotel-issued robe. "Once the snare tightens around Alexi, he'll give orders for Max to be sent back to Glazkova. And there's nothing the CIA or anyone else can do about that. Max has to be with me when Alexi goes down."

"I might be able to arrange that." Rio crossed his arms and dug his fingers into his biceps. *Why'd he go and promise that?* Ever since his mother had died, he'd vowed never to play protector again.

Tori whipped her hands out of the pockets and clapped them together. "Now we're on the same page. What do you want to know?"

Running her fingers through her curls, she dropped

onto the sofa and kicked her feet up on the coffee table.

Rio perched on the arm of the sofa and hunched forward with his hands on his knees. How exactly was he supposed to get a kid out of Alexi Zherkov's compound with its guards and motion sensors? He didn't figure Alexi would allow his son to go anywhere with his nanny without protection.

"Look, Tori…"

They both jumped at the sharp rap on the hotel door. "Room service."

Holding up his hand to Tori, Rio crept toward the door. He squinted through the peephole and assessed the waiter with the cart. He swung open the door, keeping possession of the handle in case he had to smash it against the waiter's face.

The waiter wheeled the cart into the room and hoisted a silver tray. "On the coffee table or credenza?"

"Right here." Tori patted the gleaming surface of the coffee table in front of her.

The waiter unloaded several items from the cart. "Enjoy."

Rio dug some bills from his pocket and handed them to the waiter on his way out. When he turned back to the room, Tori had already lifted the covers from two plates.

She closed her eyes and sniffed. "This smells great. Last thing I had to eat, if you can call it that, was the shaved ice. Don't get me wrong. It was exceptional, but hardly a meal."

"About getting to your son…"

She picked up a french fry and waved it in the air. "We don't need to discuss the details now. I know you can get him out."

Tori had a helluva lot more confidence in him than he did. He let out a breath and joined her on the sofa. She had one thing right. The food smelled good and his body demanded sustenance.

They ate in silence for several minutes until Tori dropped her half-eaten burger onto the plate. "Whoa. Ate too fast."

Rio touched his nose. "You have some ketchup on the tip of your nose."

She snorted and dabbed her nose with her napkin. "That's another reason why they kicked me out of Glazkova."

"How'd you wind up marrying him?"

Holding the napkin over her mouth, she slumped against the cushions of the sofa. "I was young and stupid. While I was in college, both of my parents died in a plane crash. I wanted to quit school and go home, but my brother forced me to stick with it. Once I graduated, I didn't want to go home anymore. Instead, I decided to travel."

"Glazkova?"

"Not at first. I spent time in different countries and kept hearing about Glazkova—the parties, the beaches, the lifestyle. I decided to check it out for myself."

"And was it all you dreamed it would be?" Rio cocked his head to study her face. He had a hard time imagining this single-minded woman relaxing.

"Oh, yeah." She twisted the napkin in her lap. "For the tourists anyway, there seemed to be no rules, no laws. It was one big party, presided over by the partier-in-chief, Prince Alexi."

"Were his parents already dead?" He'd heard once the old prince had died, the younger generation had let loose. Alexi's father had also been involved in criminal enterprises, but not drugs and not arms dealing.

She nodded. "They died a few years before I arrived, so party central was in full-swing."

"And you met Alexi at one of his parties?"

"Not just any party, his big birthday bash."

"What was it? Love at first sight? He swept you off your feet beneath a full Glazkova moon?" Rio's jaw tightened. For some reason that scenario left a bitter taste in his mouth.

Tori gave a short laugh and dragged a fry through a puddle of ketchup on her plate. "Not exactly."

"A slow courtship? He wined and dined you. Introduced you to the beauty of his country, the magnitude of his wealth and power?"

She compressed her lips and smashed the fry on her plate. "Not. Exactly."

The blood pumped in Rio's veins, fast and hot. Had the SOB coerced her in some way? He knew it. No chance a classy woman like Tori would fall for scum like Alexi.

Rio reached for her hand, entwining his sticky fingers with hers. "What happened, Tori? How'd you become Princess Victoria of Glazkova?"

For the second time that night, someone knocked on the hotel door. Gasping, Tori disentangled herself from Rio and jumped from the sofa. She shushed him and tripped toward the door.

Standing on tiptoes, she peeked out the peephole. Then she spun around, and with her face as white as a sandy beach, she drew her index finger across her throat.

Chapter Five

Tori's already rapidly beating heart went into full gallop when Rio charged toward the door. What exactly did he think he was going to do to Alexi in her hotel room?

She rushed at him and grabbed his forearms, the muscles corded and tight. Drawing him close, she whispered, "You can't do this now. You have to hide."

Rio huffed out a warm breath, stirring her damp hair. "I'm not leaving you alone with him."

"It's what I wanted. It's what I came for." Not that she didn't want to leave that door closed on Alexi forever and fall into this man's warm, protective embrace. But she had to get Max. Nothing else mattered. "You'll be putting me in more danger if Alexi finds you here, if he figures out who you are."

Alexi rapped on the door again. "Victoria, I know you're in there. Let me in."

Tori shoved at Rio's solid chest, although she had no idea where he could hide in the suite. His chocolate brown eyes darkened and he crushed her against his body and murmured into her hair, "Be careful."

Rio cruised past the coffee table and scooped up the extra plate and glass and then slipped through the sliding glass door.

"Just a minute. I'm here." She unlatched the chain

from the door and swept it open. It was a mistake to show any weakness in front of Alexi. He'd detect it and go in for the kill.

The lean, dark man lounging against the wall pinned her with piercing dark eyes in a craggy face. He had a few more lines than she remembered. Drugs? No, Alexi sold but never indulged. Stress. Must be nerve-racking to have to watch your back 24/7.

Her gaze slid past Alexi to the dark shape hulking in the background. She leveled a finger at the bodyguard. "He's not coming in here. He scared me spitless when he grabbed me earlier."

"Still giving orders, Victoria?" Alexi's heavy lids fell over his eyes as if she bored him already.

"Damn straight."

He raised his brows. "If you came all the way to Maui to talk to me, you can at least let me into your hotel room."

Stepping aside, she ushered him in, sweeping her arm into the room. "After you."

Alexi strolled around the room, wrinkling his nose at the tray of half-eaten food. Good thinking on Rio's part to take the extra plate and glass. She'd have had a hard time explaining the table for two to Alexi.

He plucked a napkin from the tray and wiped off the edge of the credenza before leaning his hip against its edge. "What is it you want, Victoria?"

"How's Max?"

"Maksim is fine. He's a little prince—imperious, demanding and self-confident—everything he should be."

Tori gulped against the sour bile rising from her gut. He was turning her sweet boy into a monster, just like his father. "I want to see him."

Alexi clicked his tongue while he smoothed back his hair. "You abandoned your son. You have no rights."

"We're not in Glazkova anymore." Tori clenched her fists and took a step toward Alexi.

"And that means?" He brushed an imaginary speck of lint from his black turtleneck.

"That means I can make life a living hell for you here while you're…doing business. Attorneys, court appearances, subpoenas, law enforcement."

Alexi snapped his fingers. "I can whisk Maksim back to Glazkova at a moment's notice if I choose."

Tori swallowed her fear and straightened her spine. "You may send Max back, but you'll still be here. And I'll come at you even harder."

Alexi pushed off the credenza and wandered toward the sliding door to the balcony. His eyes met hers in the reflection of the glass. "And what if I allow you to see Maksim?"

Tori shoved her hand in the deep pocket of the robe so she wouldn't smash her fist into his smug face. "If I can visit with Max while he's in Maui, I won't cause any trouble for you."

"Of course, I couldn't allow unsupervised visits." Alexi spread his hands and shrugged. "An adulterer is hardly a fit mother for my son, the future Prince of Glazkova."

Gritting her teeth, Tori smiled. "We both know the truth about that charge. However, I don't mind supervised visits. Is Irina still with you?"

He spun around to face her. "She is, but Irina is silly and sentimental. I wouldn't trust her not to fall under your persuasive spell, Victoria. After all, you bewitched me."

God, she'd love to see Rio plant his big fist against

Alexi's aristocratic nose. She lifted a shoulder. "Send a guard with us. I don't care. I just want to see my son."

"One guard? You'd probably have him wrapped around your little finger in a matter of days."

"Oh, for Pete's sake. Send an army with us." She knew darned well Alexi wouldn't want to leave her alone with Max too far out of his domain. But he had to be the one to suggest the compound. She didn't want him to suspect her eagerness to stay under his roof.

Alexi brought his hands together and rested his chin on the tips of his fingers. "I suppose if you stayed at my facility here in Maui, I might be comfortable enough."

"Stay with you? Are you nuts? I tried that once before. Didn't work out too well."

"Yes." His dark eyes glowed as he warmed up to the idea. "You could stay in the south wing of the property with Maksim, see him every day, but under the watchful eye of my staff. Take it or leave it, Victoria."

She gestured toward the double doors of her suite. "You can't send Igor out there along with me? I'm sure he'd never succumb to my feminine wiles."

"You'd have to give up this nice suite." He grabbed the handle of the sliding door and yanked it. "Such a beautiful view, but I assure you I have such views from my property."

Alexi stepped onto the balcony and Tori's heart skittered in her chest. He said something else, but he wasn't shouting so he hadn't discovered Rio yet.

"What?" She followed him outside, her gaze darting to the four corners of the empty balcony.

"I said, my view is nicer because the location is more isolated."

Where was Rio? Her suite was on the fifth floor with

nothing but ocean fronting the balcony. Did he take another dive? She shivered and hugged herself.

"Are you cold?" Alexi moved closer and she took a step back. His gaze trailed down her body and she shivered again. "You must've been in the shower when I arrived. Are you naked beneath the robe?"

She pressed her back against the balcony and clamped her arms across her waist, tugging at the robe's sash. "You *are* crazy."

He chuckled. "Don't act so shocked. I remember how hot you were. Still are."

"That's funny. I don't remember much at all about those nights in Glazkova."

"You *were* a party girl, Victoria." He winked like the one-eyed blinking of a lizard.

"And you *are* a drug dealer, Alexi. You had access to all kinds of pretty little pills, didn't you? Which one did you slip into my drink?"

He threw his head back and laughed. "Believe what you will, Victoria. You were a willing companion and we created a superior son."

"A son I never get to see." She was grateful for the darkness that shrouded the balcony and hid the tears sparkling in her eyes. She'd never allow Alexi to see her cry…ever.

Alexi jerked his head up at a scraping sound from the balcony next door. "What's that?"

"I think my neighbors opened their door and then shut it." Tori held her breath. Somehow Rio must've jumped to the next balcony.

"A suite like this should afford you more privacy. Wait until you see the compound I rented south of here."

"I'm sure it's quite a luxurious prison." She moved toward the sliding door to get Alexi off the balcony.

Alexi stepped inside after her, and she released a slow, measured breath. "You can come and go as you please. You just can't take Maksim with you when you do so. In exchange, you won't harass me with your American lawyers and writs and decrees and court appearances. You'd lose anyway."

No, you're going to lose this time, Prince Alexi.
"Fine."

He held out his hand, his long, tapered fingers almost touching her arm. "Shall we shake on it?"

"That's okay." She brushed past him on her way to the door. "Give me the directions and I'll be there tomorrow."

Alexi paused in front of the credenza and wrapped his fingers around Rio's mini wine bottle. Picking it up, he tilted it toward the other wine bottle on the coffee table. "I thought you never had more than one drink... anymore."

"I tipped that one over when I opened it and half the wine spilled out. Not that my drinking habits are your business...anymore. Tomorrow then?"

"Tomorrow isn't good." Alexi grasped the handle and opened the door, revealing his bodyguard still lounging nearby. "The day after tomorrow works better for me."

"Does Max remember me?" Tori arranged her face into a stiff mask.

Alexi's own face hardened and his black eyes narrowed to slits. "I told my son the truth. His mother abandoned him and was no longer welcome in our country. If he thinks of you at all, it's with the proper distaste."

"Have Igor leave the directions at the front desk. Same place he dropped off that rotting lei, courtesy of you. I'll drive my rental car out the day after tomorrow." She slammed the door and pressed her back against it until the sorrow overwhelmed her.

Then she sank to the floor in a boneless heap.

THE VOICES FROM TORI'S suite ceased and Rio thought he heard a door slamming. He uncurled his large frame from beneath the table shoved up against the side of the balcony. He climbed onto the side and leaped to Tori's balcony, his hands grasping for the edge. He swung to the side and hoisted his legs over, his bare feet slapping against the tile.

Peering into the room, his blood ran cold and his heart froze. He strode across the sitting room carpet and crouched next to Tori, huddled on the floor, her hair creating a veil over her face.

"Did he hurt you? I'll kill him."

She shook her head and her hair swayed. "Not physically."

All the sass had evaporated from Tori's voice, which quavered and cracked. He'd heard enough of their conversation on the balcony to figure out how that piece of garbage had coerced Tori into bed.

Rio scooped her up in his arms and carried her into the bedroom. With one hand he yanked back the covers on the king-size bed and settled her on the satin sheets. Then he tucked the top sheet and blanket around her body, curled away from him in a fetal position.

He sat on the edge of the bed and held her hand between his, rubbing her stiff fingers. He wanted to comfort her but he didn't have the words. He couldn't express his thoughts, which swirled in the violence he wanted to inflict on that man.

So he held her hand.

After several minutes, she sniffled and stirred. "Sorry," she mumbled into the pillow.

"Don't be."

Rolling toward him, she brushed the curls from her face. He'd expected wet cheeks and a red nose, but she hadn't shed any tears. Her freckles stood out on her pale skin, and she blinked her glassy eyes a few times.

"What did he say to hurt you?" More like devastated, judging from her demeanor.

"Does it matter? It's all one big pile of hurt."

"I can take some of that hurt if you want to share it with me." He'd had enough pain in his lifetime—he could shoulder hers without reaching his own threshold.

She gripped his hand like a lifeline. "He's been telling lies about me to Max. M-Max hates me now."

He circled his thumb against the back of her hand. At least his mother never bad-mouthed Ralph McClintock to him. He'd learned to hate the man all on his own. "Max doesn't hate you. How old is he—five?"

"Four."

"A four-year-old needs his mother. He may agree with his father because he wants to please him, but Max doesn't hate you. Whatever lies Alexi has fed him, Max will forgive anything. You're his mom."

The corner of Tori's mouth lifted. "Never figured you for a pop psychologist. That was pretty good."

Warmth washed over his face, and he shrugged. "I have a lot of experience with weird family dynamics and an absent parent."

Tori glanced down at their entwined hands. "Thanks, Rio."

"I overheard a little of your conversation on the balcony. Did Alexi slip you a date rape drug in Glazkova?"

A rose color flooded her pale cheeks. "I—I'm not sure. To his credit and my discredit, it's not like he beat me over the head and dragged me off to his bed."

He shrugged. The last thing he wanted to do was make her feel guilty about bad choices…or hear about her courtship with Alexi. "I didn't figure Prince Alexi would have to use those methods with any woman."

"No." She ran her hands over her face. "He had charm to spare, believe it or not. He was everything a girl from the sticks dreamed of—urbane, sophisticated, cultured and knowledgeable about art and music and literature. A real catch if you never saw his dark side."

He cocked his head. How did a girl from the sticks manage to get invited to parties thrown by Glazkova royalty?

"When did you get your first hint of his dark side?"

"Pretty soon after I met him. A tiger can't hide his stripes for too long. He was possessive and jealous, so I tread warily and didn't plan to get in too deep."

"And then he drugged you?"

"I don't know." She slipped her hand from his and fluffed up her hair, the life and sparkle returning to her eyes. "I couldn't prove a thing. I partied along with everyone else and wound up in Alexi's bed. Then I wound up pregnant."

"Let me guess. Alexi changed when you got pregnant."

Tori nodded. "He became the model companion and father-to-be and swept me off my feet. He explained that it would be shameful for him to have a child out of wedlock in his country, so he proposed."

"There's one thing I don't get." Rio hoisted himself across the foot of the bed and rested his head on his hand. "Don't get me wrong, you're a gorgeous woman, but why did Alexi set his sights on you? He couldn't find some attractive, willing Glazkovian woman to marry and have his children?"

Snorting, Tori folded her hands behind her head and gazed at the ceiling. "The Glazkovians are a superstitious people, and Mad Prince Alexi buys into all the myths. His grandmother was some kind of gypsy seer and filled Alexi's head with the old legends."

"What do those old legends and myths have to do with you?" Rio dug his elbow into the bed. This story became more and more fascinating, kind of like Tori herself. He'd be wise to follow Tori's advice to herself: tread warily and don't get in too deep.

Tori tipped her chin down and raised one brow. "Are you ready for this? His grandmother told him when he was a child that he had to marry a red-haired, green-eyed foreigner who would then bear him a firstborn son. This son would lead Glazkova to greatness in the next century."

Rio's jaw dropped. The Prince of Glazkova really was mad, and he must've inherited his insanity from his grandmother. "You're not kidding, are you?"

"Nope."

"So when you, with your red hair and green eyes, traipsed into Glazkova, Alexi had to have you...by hook or by crook."

"Exactly. I had no idea what kind of crazy trap I was walking into when I traveled to that country. When I got pregnant so quickly and then had a son, that sealed the deal for Alexi. He knew he'd made the right decision."

Rio squeezed Tori's ankle through the bed covers. "Alexi made the right decision, but the situation couldn't have worked out any worse for you."

Tori kicked out, nailing him in the thigh with her heel,

and shoved up to a seated position. "How can you say that? Regardless of how things worked out with Alexi, I have my son. I have Max."

Her words twisted a knife in his gut. Maybe his own mother had regarded his existence as a mistake, but Tori didn't feel that way about her son.

Tori looked at him with something akin to loathing, her green eyes narrow like a cat's, a cat waiting to pounce. Rio hoisted himself beside her and brushed his fingers along her arm.

"I'm sorry. Stupid thing to say."

Her shoulders slumped. "I know what you meant. I'm still on edge after Alexi's visit. I—I'm glad you were outside. It made me feel safer."

She reached out a hand and skimmed his unshaven chin with her knuckles. Her eyes, which had been as hard as glass, softened.

Rio captured her wrist and kissed the center of her palm where he felt her pulse beating against his lips. She shifted her position, curling her legs beneath her and leaning toward him.

He'd wanted to taste her again ever since their make-believe kiss on the sidewalk. Curling his fingers around hers, he tucked her hand against his chest as he pulled her close. He brushed her bottom lip with his, and her mouth parted. He laid a path of kisses along her jaw and whispered in her ear. "I'll help you any way I can, Tori."

She let out a long sigh and closed her eyes. "I'm sure glad to hear you say that, Rio, because I'm moving into Alexi's compound the day after tomorrow and I'm ready to start spying on that SOB."

Chapter Six

The warm breath that had been tickling her ear turned into a hiss. Rio jerked back and dropped her hand.

"You're what?"

Tori peeled one eyelid open. "Moving into the compound. Don't worry. Alexi assured me it's a lot more luxurious than this dump."

Rio bounded from the bed and clutched his dark hair, already a tousled mess. "Why are you putting yourself in danger? I told you to stay out of there."

"That's why Alexi was here." Leaning back against the padded headboard, Tori folded her hands in her lap. "I thought you'd figured that out. I told Alexi's minion that I wanted to talk to Alexi, and he wasted no time getting over here. Of course, I let Alexi believe the invitation to his compound originated with him. He won't suspect a thing."

Rio paced across the floor and pounded the wall with his fist. "You're putting yourself in the line of fire. He's a drug dealer, Tori, and an arms dealer now. What if one of his enemies decides to raid his compound while you're staying there?"

"Then I'll be in a better position to protect my son." She crossed her legs at the ankle and tapped her feet together. Rio really didn't understand maternal bonding at all. What kind of woman did old Ralph McClintock knock up thirty years ago? Boy, could Ralph pick 'em. Rio's half brothers' mom was no Mother of the Year either.

"Wait. We're close to bringing Alexi down. When that happens, you'll get Max."

"Bull." She leveled a finger at him. "You guys don't have a thing. You never have and you never will if you continue to play by the same old rules. You said you wanted someone on the inside. I'm your mole."

"You're not a mole. You're a mother."

"That's even better."

Rio slapped his palm against his forehead. "What are you talking about?"

"Alexi knows I'm focused on being with Max. He'd never imagine I'd be up to anything else in that house."

"How do you know that for sure? He's jumpy, edgy."

Shrugging, Tori threw back the bed covers and swung her legs off the side of the bed. "Alexi thinks women are stupid. He tricked me so easily, he doesn't see me as a threat. I'm an annoyance, and he figures the fastest way to stop my interference is to throw me a bone and let me see Max while he's in Hawaii."

"It's dangerous, Tori." Rio sank on the bed next to her and gripped her shoulders.

She turned to face him, her hair trailing across his wrists. "A lot of things are dangerous, cowboy."

Dropping her gaze to Rio's sensuous mouth, she ran her tongue along her bottom lip. Could they just share one kiss that wasn't a fake or didn't get interrupted? If she planned to go into the lion's den and face Alexi, she needed a little sustenance first.

Rio curled his hand around her neck. "You like playing with fire, don't you?"

"Let's just say I'll do what it takes to get my son back."

"How do you know you can trust me?" He dropped his thumb to the hollow of her throat and she swallowed.

She almost told him her trust came from the fact that she would put her life in the hands of any McClintock from Silverhill, Colorado. But she didn't want to complicate the situation. Instead she batted her eyelashes. "I know I can trust you because I've been stark naked under this robe since I got out of the shower, and you've hardly made a move."

"You mean like this?" He tucked his hands beneath the collar of her robe where they scorched her back, and then bent his head, taking her mouth in a possessive kiss.

Her teasing had ignited a full-blown conflagration. Rio edged one hand to the back of her head, grabbing her hair as he angled his lips across hers for a more thorough assault. Her hands fisted the material of his T-shirt as she held on for support.

Rio tasted of the sea and ruby red wine and all that was dark and forbidden and delicious.

He leaned against her, pushing her back onto the pillows, wedging his muscular thigh against hers. She needed more contact, so she entwined her arms around his neck. The kiss deepened, binding her more closely to this man...her savior of the evening.

The tie on her robe loosened. Rio's lips left hers and trailed down her throat. She released his shoulders to wrench open her robe. Then she slid off the bed and landed on the floor at Rio's bare feet.

Tori scrambled to her knees. Not so overcome by

passion that he couldn't see the humor in her tumble, Rio threw his head back and laughed.

Glancing down, Tori gasped at the one exposed breast. It was one thing flashing your breast at a man kissing your neck, quite another to flash a man wiping his eyes with tears of laughter.

She yanked her robe closed and crossed her arms. "All right, it wasn't that funny. Did I completely ruin the moment?"

"I'm sorry. Are you okay?" He hitched his hands under her arms and dragged her into his lap.

That's better. She snuggled in closer to his broad chest and inhaled his thoroughly male scent.

He shuddered and yanked the collar of her robe together. "Tori, that fall just saved us from a big mistake."

She stopped wriggling. "You seem to think everything's a mistake. You use that word a lot."

He wrapped her hair around his hand. "You have the false idea that getting closer to me will ensure my cooperation in your harebrained scheme to bring down Alexi Zherkov."

"That's not why I..."

He put his finger over her lips, still throbbing from his powerful kiss. "It's the opposite. If you were truly my woman, there's no way in hell I'd let you go into that nest of vipers."

His woman. She sagged against him. He still had her pegged as a user, and he'd let her go to Alexi freely. Isn't that what she wanted?

Lucky for her, she'd never be Rio McClintock's woman.

Gulping back the lump in her throat, she slipped from his lap. "Well, I'm not your woman."

Rio stood up and stretched, displaying ripples of hard muscle and smooth, bronzed skin. "If I can't talk you out of your plan, let me make my position clear. I don't expect, nor do I want any insider information from you. So visit with your son and then get out. I'll make sure the CIA notifies you when we bring down your ex-husband."

Cruising into the sitting room, Tori called over her shoulder, "Whatever. You can leave now."

As she approached the hotel room door and grasped the handle, Rio appeared behind her. He wedged his hand against the door. "Wait."

She closed her eyes as he bent closer, her breath coming out in little puffs. Maybe he'd changed his mind. Maybe his desire had overruled his thick skull and he'd toss her over his shoulder and carry her back to the bedroom.

"All clear."

Her eyelids flew open. Rio's face was against the door, his eye at the peephole. His rejection hit her like a bucket of salt water.

With his brow furrowed, he cocked his head. "Are you okay? Nobody's waiting in the hallway."

Nobody was waiting in her bed either.

"You still here? I'm just swell."

He grinned and opened the door a crack. Satisfied by what he saw, or didn't see, in the entrance area to the suites, he stepped across the threshold.

Before Tori could slam the door on his backside, he swung around and pinched her chin between his thumb and index finger. "What's your last name anyway? I usually don't kiss a woman until I've been properly introduced."

"Aren't you the gentleman? Scott. My name's Tori Scott."

"Pleasure to meet you." He leaned forward, planted a hard kiss on her mouth and turned away.

As Tori shut the door, still dazed by his parting salute, she thought she heard him whisper, "If you were my woman."

THE FOLLOWING AFTERNOON Rio shook out the newspaper and adjusted his sunglasses. The Agency would have a fit when he submitted his receipts for this job. He couldn't help it. The ex-Mrs. Alexi Zherkov had expensive tastes. He had to check into her hotel to stay close to her.

And he wanted to stay close to her.

"Another club soda, sir?"

The flower behind the ear of the poolside cocktail waitress floated onto his chaise lounge as she dipped to pick up his empty glass.

He twirled the stem of the flower between his fingers as he held it out to her. "Lost something."

She grinned and rolled her eyes. "That always happens. Keep it. I'll get another at the bar. Drink?"

"Sure. Make it a mai tai this time." Hell, he deserved a vacation and a fruity drink with an umbrella. Seems like he'd been all around the world chasing Alexi Zherkov since he took his last vacation.

His last vacation.

Not that he'd call a visit to Colorado to square things away with his older half brother a vacation. Thinking about Rod McClintock as his half brother always gave him a jolt. Rio and his mother had been on their own so long, he didn't give family a second thought. But he had one…a big one. Not one, but three half brothers, their assorted wives and children, a father and a stepmother. He had no clue who else lurked in the vast McClintock lineage, and he had no interest in finding out.

When the waitress returned with his drink, Rio's gaze locked on to the redhead with the straw cowboy hat and bulging bag over her shoulder. Finally.

Rio hoped he could count on Tori not to make a big deal over his appearance on the pool deck at her hotel. She scanned the patio and swiveled her head back in his direction. He slid the newspapers from the lounge next to his and hoped she'd get the hint.

She got it.

Tori scuffed across the deck in a pair of flip-flops with pink plastic flowers between the toes. She gripped the back of the chaise lounge.

"Is someone sitting here?"

"No. My wife is up in our room recovering from a nasty hangover." He held up his mai tai. "Too many of these at the luau."

The waitress hovered between them. "Can I get you a drink?"

"Just a diet soda, please." She dropped her bag on the foot of the chaise. "I don't want to suffer the same fate as his wife."

As the waitress wandered away to take another order, Tori lowered her voice. "What are you doing at my hotel?"

"It's my hotel now."

"Are you spying on me?"

"Protecting you."

"I'm not in any danger."

"Not yet."

She rummaged through her beach bag and pulled out a book and a bottle of sunscreen...SPF fifty-five.

Rio pointed to the orange bottle. "What's the point of sitting in the sun when you have that slathered all over you?"

"If I don't use a strong sunblock I'll burn to a crisp, but I still like sitting in the sun." She squirted a puddle of white lotion into the palm of her hand. "Some of us are not bronzed gods...or goddesses."

Tori rubbed the sunblock onto her shapely calf and then yanked her white, gauzy cover-up over her head, exposing her tiny red bikini. Rio swallowed hard and took a long sip from his drink.

Tori may not be bronzed, but she definitely nailed the goddess label.

"I'm Mexican."

"Huh?"

"I'm half-Mexican. That's why I tan so easily."

She carefully lifted the strap of her bikini top and spread the lotion along her shoulder. "Your mother is Mexican?"

"Yeah, how'd you guess that?"

"You told me your last name, McClintock. Remember? Unless that's not your real name."

"That's it." Sitting forward, he straddled his chaise lounge. "Do you think your ex-husband is having you watched?"

She shoved her big sunglasses to the tip of her nose and surveyed the pool area. "No. He knows what I'm doing here now, and he'll expect me to show up tomorrow."

"You're still determined to do so?"

"Of course. In fact, I'm glad you're here. It gives us an opportunity to discuss our plan."

He collapsed back against the chaise lounge and

sighed. That red hair must come with a stubborn streak. "I told you. We don't have a plan."

"Exactly. That's why we need one."

"I don't want you gathering information about Alexi." For all his tough talk last night about forbidding her to go to the compound, Rio realized he could no sooner stop Tori from seeing her son than he could stop a typhoon from hitting Maui. Whether she belonged to him or not.

"It's not up to you, Rio. Once I deliver the goods, you'll change your mind." She adjusted her hat to shade her face and folded open her paperback.

"I'm not making any deals with you, Tori. I'm not having that on my conscience." She ignored him and buried her nose farther in her book.

After several minutes of silence, Tori thumped the book on her knee, and then held it up for him to see. "It's all in here."

Rio squinted at the thick spy novel. "What's in there?"

"Lots and lots of plans." She tilted the book back and forth in front of her face. "We can have a secret meeting place or a spot to leave messages for each other. I could flash lights from the compound when I have information."

He snorted. "Or you could just call me from your cell phone. How many of those books have you been reading lately?"

"Enough to get me well versed in spy tactics. Alexi may not be following me now, but once I'm in his sphere he'll probably have his goons trail me from the compound if only to make sure I'm not stealing something, including Max. He may even confiscate my phone. So we need to have a way to communicate."

Tori thumbed through the pages as if doing research instead of reading a beach book. Her index finger skimmed along the lines of the book and then she tapped the page. "Here's an idea. We can use a tree."

Rio stretched and snapped open his newspaper. "You leave a mark on a predesignated tree and place your information under a rock or tucked inside a bush."

"How'd you know that?" She tipped down her glasses to study him.

"It's a common CIA method." He shrugged. Did Tori really believe she'd have time to snoop around and get something on Alexi? She'd be too busy reuniting with her son…and that's how it should be.

"The tree in that little park by the shaved ice place should work. There are plenty of bushes around there, and I could probably hide something in one of them."

"Tori, you need to stop. I already told you, I don't want you nosing around Alexi's business. It's dangerous and he's dangerous. You're not his favorite person as it is."

"You underestimate me, cowboy."

Rio didn't underestimate her one bit, least of all the power she wielded over him. He clenched his jaw as his gaze raked over her luscious curves. Her body held only a fraction of the pull he felt like a tidal wave. Her fierce loyalty and determination transformed her into an unstoppable force that swept along everything in its path.

The Hawaiian sun, the rum and his proximity to this woman had him hot and bothered. He needed several cold showers and a refocus on his work.

"I'm going to take a swim in the ocean." He folded

his paper and laid it on his chaise lounge. "If the waitress ever returns, order me a club soda, lots of ice."

He scooped up the fragrant orchid the waitress dropped and tucked it behind Tori's ear, his fingers trailing down her neck. Cool down. Ocean. Now.

She grinned as if reading his thoughts. "You go take that dip, and I'll search this book for more tips."

TORI WATCHED RIO STRIDE across the pool deck to the sandy beach, his muscled back flaring into a set of broad shoulders, his long black hair swinging with each confident step. Hers weren't the only eyes that followed his progress. Several women peered over their magazines, sucking on their straws as they watched him jog out to the beach.

Sighing, she dropped her book. Just her luck to run into a man like Rio when she had so many other priorities on her plate. She didn't have time to rescue her son and lust after a man at the same time.

She bit her lip. *Who are you kidding, Tori?* The danger of her predicament only heightened her attraction to Rio. She'd always preferred her men with a dash of excitement thrown in to fan the flames.

She reached for her glass and a shadow fell across her upper body. Shading her eyes, she twisted around and choked. The man from last night and another bodybuilder type, incongruous in shorts and flip-flops, hovered over her chaise lounge.

The hairy one peeled his lips back into a semblance of a smile. "It's time to leave now, Princess Victoria."

Her gaze darted toward the beach where Rio had just disappeared and back to the man's face. "What are you doing here? I'm supposed to drive over tomorrow."

"Change of plans. Prince Alexi wants you at the

compound now." He scooped her cover-up out of her bag and tossed it onto her stomach. "Let's go."

She licked her lips. Better to leave before Rio came back. Although Igor looked stupid, even he might put two and two together and wonder why she was sitting poolside with the man who had come to her rescue last night.

"All right. Don't get pushy." She pulled her cover-up over her body, stuffed her feet into her sandals and grabbed her bag.

As she turned toward the path that led to the elevators, the man grabbed her arm. "You're coming with us now."

"My room's that way." She pointed toward the spa.

"You're not going to your room. Prince Alexi ordered us to take you directly to the compound. He'll send someone for your things later."

She narrowed her eyes and jerked from his grasp. Why had she trusted Alexi? He always used the element of surprise to keep her off kilter. "And if I refuse to go with you today?"

He lifted his big shoulders. "You don't see Prince Maksim."

Butterflies took flight in her belly, and she pivoted toward the lobby feeling like a prisoner between Alexi's two henchmen. She glanced over her shoulder at the beach.

Would she ever see Rio again?

Chapter Seven

On his way to the beach, Rio took a detour by the towel kiosk and picked up a beach towel. He dashed across the hot sand and waded into the water. The lukewarm temperature didn't have the same bracing effect as the chilly Pacific off the coast of California, but it would do in a pinch.

He dove under the small rolling waves and flipped onto his back. He had to get Alexi. Tori deserved a chance with her son. Once the CIA arrested her ex, they'd have to move fast to recover Max.

Although Rio had assured Tori that the CIA could stop Alexi from sending Max back to Glazkova after his arrest, he didn't have as much confidence in that scenario as he pretended.

After he swam about a hundred yards back and forth in the calm ocean, Rio headed for shore. Maybe if they could find an out-of-the-way place and make sure they weren't followed, he and Tori could have dinner tonight before she got sucked into Alexi's sphere.

Then what, McClintock? Get carried away again with the ex-wife of your current prey?

He snatched up his towel from the sand and shook out his hair. He cranked on the shower that perched at the edge of the sand, separating the beach from the hotel.

Sluicing the cool water across his skin, he rinsed the salt water from his body.

He slung the towel over one shoulder and strode up the path back to the pool area. A furrow formed between his eyebrows as he dropped his towel on the back of Tori's chaise lounge, vacant save for the purple orchid on the center of her towel. His gaze zigzagged back and forth across the pool and bar.

"Looking for your friend?"

His head jerked toward the waitress, balancing another tray on the inside of her forearm. "Yeah. Did she head for the water?"

"No." She placed a club soda on the glass table next to his seat. "They left."

Rio's heart picked up speed. "They?"

"She and the two big guys who escorted her out of the hotel."

AT THE CURB, TORI TRIED to shake off the man gripping her upper arm. "Back off."

"Don't make a scene, or you'll never see Prince Maksim again."

The man's low growl sent a spiral of fear to her belly. She took a deep breath. "Why can't I go back to my room and pack a bag? This is ridiculous. I'm wearing a bikini, flip-flops and a flimsy cover-up."

The man shrugged. "Prince Alexi will send someone to pick up your things."

"What is he afraid of? Does he think I'll pack a gun and take Max by force?"

Her captor barked out a laugh. "Prince Alexi doesn't fear you, but he doesn't want you calling the shots. He decides when and how you'll come to the compound, not you."

Tori snorted. "Control freak."

The other man, the one with no neck and apparently no voice, opened the back door of the limo waiting at the curb. Before he pushed her inside, she twisted her head around for a last desperate glimpse of Rio. Would he figure out what had happened to her? She had her cell phone with her, and although she didn't have his number, she could reach him at the hotel now that he'd taken up residence there.

The men slammed the door on her, and she immediately tried the handle. Locked. She scrambled across the leather seat and grabbed the other handle. That proved fruitless. They'd locked her into the back of the limo.

Screaming in frustration she kicked out at the tinted security glass that separated her from the thugs who had kidnapped her. The big car lurched away from the curb, and she fell across the seat. She pulled herself upright and snapped on her seat belt.

Actually she'd lucked out that Rio had been at the beach when the two nightmares in aloha shirts appeared at the pool. One of the thugs who'd grabbed her was Igor from the night before. He would've recognized Rio, and then she'd have had a lot of explaining to do.

While Tori dug into her beach bag with one hand, scrambling for her cell phone, she cupped the other hand against the security glass and tried to peer into the front seat. A voice blared from the speaker to her left, and she jumped.

"Do you need something, Princess Victoria?"

So much for calling the hotel. If the matching goons had orders to watch her, they'd never allow her to make a call, or at least they'd be listening in on her conversation. But she had to try. She held up her cell phone. "Can I make a call?"

The glass where her hand was still resting slid down and the man in the passenger seat leaned his head into the back of the car, smiling. "Of course you can make a call. You're not a prisoner."

"He speaks. I'm not a prisoner, huh?" She tried the unyielding doors. "You could've fooled me."

She sucked in her lower lip and rubbed her thumb across the smooth surface of her phone. If only she knew Rio's room number, at least she could leave a message with some kind of gibberish or some code. But she didn't, and she couldn't very well ask the front desk for his number with Alexi's men listening and taking notes.

The driver mumbled something and the man in the passenger seat snatched the phone from Tori's hand. "Hey, I thought you just said I wasn't a prisoner."

He shrugged as he pocketed her phone. "Change of plans."

"Plans sure change a lot around here." She jerked away as the glass slid back into place. *Smart move, Tori.* She should've just kept the phone a secret. Now she had no opportunity to use it.

Slumping back against the seat, she curled her legs beneath her. She'd think of some way to get information out to Rio, and then she'd ask for payment.

Rescue Max.

About an hour later, the limo began cruising uphill, craggy cliffs dropping off to the ocean below. She knew this part of the ocean well—she'd jumped into it only yesterday.

She'd been confident she'd encounter Ryder McClintock in Maui and he'd rush to her rescue and save Max. Instead of Ryder's sunny disposition and blond good looks, she'd run smack up against Rio's brooding intensity and dark handsomeness. And she couldn't convince him to rush into anything.

Not even bed.

The car continued curving upward where abundant vegetation now stingily afforded glimpses of the shining blue jewel of the Pacific. Alexi had ensconced himself in a private location...and a secure one. There would be no approaching this place by land.

Large gates swung open and the limo passed through, brushing close to a man toting a machine gun across his body. Tori gasped and clutched the edge of the seat. She remembered Rio's warning. Alexi had amped up his operations since she had left him.

Her stomach churned as the big, black car took her closer and closer to her son. Would Max remember her? Had Alexi poisoned him so thoroughly he'd reject her on sight?

The car door swung open and Tori wiped her palms on the cotton material of her cover-up before unsnapping her seatbelt. She hitched her bag over her shoulder and glared at the man holding the door open for her. "I want my phone back."

The man affixed his gaze on a point just beyond her shoulder, his eyes dull beneath heavy lids. He knew his place as one of Alexi's robots. Alexi paid the people in his employ well, but he also controlled them through fear and intimidation—just like his family members, including his wife.

The house before her gleamed with white marble, a perfect shell curving along the cliffs of the coastline. Her glimpses of the palatial estate from the water and Rio's perch didn't prepare her for its magnificence.

She stumbled on the drive, and one of the several thugs littering the driveway grabbed her arm. When she tried to shake him off, he smiled. "I'm Ivan. I'll be your... companion during your stay with Prince Alexi."

More like jailer. Gritting her teeth, Tori jerked her arm out of his grasp. "I don't need a companion."

Ivan touched her shoulder. "Come this way. Prince Alexi will explain the rules of your visit."

As she climbed the steps to the massive double doors pressed with gold leaf, the other men on the driveway cast curious glances her way. She recognized a few from her years in Glazkova and others must be new recruits. Their relatives back home would be so proud of their sons working for the royal family of Glazkova, even though every one of them knew the Zherkovs held their power through corruption and criminal activities.

Which was more than she had known when she got involved with Alexi. Her family had always warned her to be more circumspect, to use better judgment, to look before she leaped into the abyss. But she'd never listened. Her brother, Jared, refused to help her now. He blamed her flightiness for their parents' deaths.

The double doors swung open, and Tori's flip-flops slapped against the marble tile that covered the foyer. Her companion edged in front of her and said, "Follow me."

Trailing after his broad back, she studied the layout of the entryway—a curving staircase to the left, a short hallway that led to a set of double doors, a step-down great room with a patio and a green lawn that rolled out toward the ocean.

The huge Christmas tree in the corner of the great room gave her hope. If Alexi planned to stay here through Christmas, she'd have a few weeks to formulate a plan.

Ivan stopped in front of another set of double doors to the right and knocked.

Alexi called out, "Enter."

When she'd met Alexi, his manners had charmed and overwhelmed her. Now his pretentiousness irritated the hell out of her. Who said *enter* these days?

They walked into the room and Tori's feet sank into thick carpet. No view of the Pacific from here. Heavy drapes concealed the long windows, and dark bookshelves lined three walls with a maroon-and-gold tapestry hanging behind the desk where Alexi sprawled in a leather chair. Another man sat at attention across the desk, his startling white hair almost glowing in the dim room.

Alexi steepled his fingers, a slow smile spreading across his face as his gaze tracked over her body. "I see my men followed my orders well."

Tori swung her bag across her chest and folded her arms over it. "I don't understand why I couldn't go back to my room, shower and pack. Why didn't you just call and let me know you were sending Igor and another henchman to pick me up?"

Alexi laughed. "His name's not Igor. That was Ilya and Anton was riding shotgun, and I see you've met Ivan."

"I'm sure Ivan is a load of laughs, but I don't need a jailer."

"Vlad." Alexi nodded to the man perched on the edge of his chair. "Wait for me outside the library."

As Vlad clicked the door behind him, Alexi sat forward in his chair and leaned his elbows on the desk. "I've assigned Ivan to you for your protection and the protection of my son."

"I don't need protection. I need my clothes."

Alexi narrowed his dark eyes to slits. "I took you by

surprise because I didn't want you to prepare for anything."

Tori's pulse quickened and she felt light-headed. Did Alexi suspect her of plotting to take Max? She'd been counting on his opinion of her as a dumb female to implement her plan.

"Well, you're right." She tossed her hair and pouted. "I didn't get to prepare by taking a shower or getting my nails done or doing any shopping."

"You'll have plenty of time to get all that done here. Give me your hotel key. I'll have someone pick up your things." He extended his hand, palm up.

Tori's brow furrowed as she dug through her beach bag for her key card. She hoped Alexi's gofer didn't run across Rio skulking around her hotel room.

She pulled the card from her bag and approached the mahogany desk. She dropped the key card on the surface of the desk, avoiding Alexi's hand. "Oops."

He peeled the card from the desk blotter and slid it into the pocket of his black slacks. "I instructed Ivan to bring you to me first so we can review the house rules. Anton confiscated your cell phone and it will remain with me for the duration of your stay. I'm conducting important, private business in this house and I don't need people wandering around the complex with private cell phones. Your phone will be returned to you when you leave."

Tori swallowed. Now she couldn't call Rio. She'd have to rely on some secret way to pass him information, but with no way to contact him, how could she let him know? Would he remember their conversation about the tree in the park? They'd never agreed on that arrangement, but at least they'd discussed it.

Alexi stood up and placed his palms on the desktop,

hunching over slightly. "Your room is next to Maksim's room, and you may visit with him as much as you like. If you wish to take him on outings, you must be accompanied by both his nanny, Irina, and Ivan."

"Hope you can keep up with us, Ivan." She backed up and out of the range of Alexi's musky cologne and nudged the big man in the ribs. Ivan's eyebrows shot up to his bald pate.

"You'll have to excuse my ex-wife, Ivan." Alexi straightened up and slicked back the sides of his black hair. "She's rather…irreverent and flighty."

That's right, Alexi. You just keep believing that. "I don't get all the cloak-and-dagger stuff. I realize I wouldn't get one mile if I snatched Max."

"I'm glad you acknowledge my power, Victoria. However, you've never been immune to realizing a truth and then acting against that truth. I don't trust you."

"And I don't trust you."

He shrugged. "That doesn't concern me. To continue with the house rules, I'll be hosting several social events and you're welcome to attend if you like. I'll also be throwing a big Christmas party before I return to Glazkova, but you aren't on the guest list for that one."

He probably planned to banish her from the house before then. She rolled her eyes. "Like I want to mingle with you and your lowlife guests at Christmas. Can't think of anything less likely to put me in the Christmas spirit."

"Do you understand the rules, Victoria?" His smooth voice held an undercurrent of malice, causing a ripple of fear along her spine. The last time she broke Prince Alexi's rules, she lost her son. This time she planned to break every rule in his black book, but the outcome would be different.

This time she had Rio McClintock on her side.

"Yeah, yeah, I understand. Now where's my son?"

Alexi pointed to the door of the library. "Take her to Maksim and stay with them. Also, send Vlad back in here."

Ivan cupped her elbow and she shrugged him off. "I can walk on my own, thanks."

She followed Ivan up the sweeping staircase on shaky legs. The meeting with her son terrified her more than the meeting with her ex. She knew what to expect from Alexi, and the man hadn't changed. She had no idea what to expect from Max.

Ivan stopped in front of a door at the end of the hallway and knocked.

A woman's voice sang out, "Come in."

Ivan pushed open the door and ushered Tori through first. Tori clutched her hands in front of her, running her tongue across her dry lips.

A beam of sunlight streamed through the window, igniting the red hair of the boy playing with Legos in the corner, his back to the door.

Irina, his nanny, rose from her chair, sliding a finger between the pages of her book. "Good afternoon, Princess Victoria. It's so good to see you again."

Tori held her breath, hoping Irina wouldn't say anything to indicate the two of them had been in contact.

Irina's gaze slid past Tori's shoulder to Ivan. "It's been a very long time."

Tori nodded and took a few halting steps toward Max. It took every ounce of steel in her gut to keep from swooping down on him and sweeping him up in her arms. She cleared her throat. "Max, Maksim?"

Her son twisted his head around, and his freckled face scrunched into a fierce scowl.

RIO CURSED AND SMACKED his palm against the valet parking desk. His gaze narrowed as he watched the black limo screech around the corner.

He should've known Prince Alexi had agreed too easily and readily to Tori's request for a visit with her son. What the hell did that maniac have planned for Tori in his oh-so-private villa? Rio didn't trust him. Alexi drugged Tori once. Who would prevent him from doing it again?

Rio grimaced. *You, cowboy.*

He turned and stalked toward one of the activity desks in the lobby. Wedging his hands on top of the desk, he leaned forward. "I need to rent a boat."

The agent's eyes widened, and she pressed into her chair as she shuffled some brochures.

Rio took a deep breath and dropped into the chair. "I'd like to take a boat out. Can you book that for me?"

The woman's shoulders slumped, and she smiled. "Of course. Are you a guest at the hotel?"

"Yes." He snapped his key card on the glass in front of her.

Her smile widened. "Would you be interested in a tour of our timeshare…?"

"No."

She jumped at the one-syllable response, and then her fingers danced through a stack of vertical files. "All right then. Let's find you that boat."

Two hours later, Rio cut the engine on his rented fishing boat and set up two poles without bait over the side. He sure hoped no Hawaiian fish would be dumb enough to bite. He dug a pair of binoculars out of his backpack and settled next to one of the fishing poles with Tori's paperback open on his knees.

She'd left in such a hurry, she'd forgotten it.

Rio trained the binoculars on the estate that gleamed white against the black-and-red volcanic cliffs. He hadn't yet watched Alexi's compound from the water, figuring Alexi's security would spot him, but he didn't have a choice now. He could view the south side of the property only from the water, and he knew Tori would be on that side with her son.

Unless Alexi had taken her somewhere else.

Rio clenched his hands tighter around the binoculars. He should've never left Tori alone. He probably knew better than she did that her ex had the power and resources to do just about whatever he pleased.

No, she'd lost her son. She knew.

After sweeping the lenses along the façade of the compound, Rio zeroed in on a large balcony that looked as if a gate or some kind of netting ringed it. The material covered the spaces between the slats of wood on the balcony—so a child couldn't squeeze through.

A bright red object rolled across that balcony...probably a ball. That must be Max's room, and if Alexi's men had taken Tori back to the compound, that's where Rio would find her.

"Come on, princess. Show your pretty face."

For the next hour, Rio bobbed on the ocean, dividing his time between checking the balcony of the compound, slathering sunblock on his body and flipping through Tori's book. The author got a lot right about the spy business...except the boredom.

Rio tossed down the book and stretched. He yanked the binoculars up and focused on the balcony for about the hundredth time. His pulse ticked up a notch when the sliding door caught a glint of sunlight.

A redhead stepped onto the balcony, and Rio let out a long breath. At least he now knew Tori's whereabouts for sure…and she looked okay—no stumbling, no lurching. No child.

She crossed her arms on the edge of the balcony and gazed at the horizon. Could she see his boat? Even if she could, she'd have no way of knowing whether or not he occupied it. He could wave his arms, but he'd be taking a big risk. He had no idea if other binoculars watched him from the estate.

Now what? He'd already called the hotel asking for any messages. Nobody had tried to contact him. Tori either didn't have use of her cell phone, or she'd had no opportunity to use it.

Rio wanted to be able to give her a heads-up when he got anything on Alexi. That way, she could prepare, be on her guard. Maybe even get Max out of there.

Who was he kidding? Alexi wouldn't allow Tori to walk out of that compound and take Max with her. Someone would have to snatch Max by force, even if the CIA did take down his father.

And Tori had already decided that Rio should do the snatching.

Tori seemed to be staring at his boat. She glanced over her shoulder into the room and then jerked up her arm. Sweet. She saw him.

He didn't dare wave back. Instead, he dropped the binoculars and grabbed a fishing pole. He reeled up the line, and then swung it over his head a few times before casting. Would Tori understand his gesture? Realize he'd seen her and acknowledged her presence?

Sure she would. She read spy novels.

With the baitless pole back in the water, Rio scooped up the binoculars again. He trained them on the now-empty balcony. What happened? Did someone catch her?

His heart thudded in his chest. He wouldn't know a

moment's peace as long as Tori remained in that criminal's home. He wouldn't rest until she left the compound and came back to him...back to his arms.

Now that he knew Alexi had taken Tori to the compound instead of drugging her and dumping her somewhere or shipping her back to Glazkova, Rio had to get back to work. He had to turn over information to the CIA that would cripple Alexi and thwart his criminal enterprise.

Maybe he could even find a way onto the compound. The estate must employ gardeners and other staff, workers that Alexi didn't personally hire and oversee. Once inside, he could scope out the security and get familiar with the layout of the grounds.

Then Rio could rescue both Tori and Max.

He yanked the binoculars over his head, stuffed them in his backpack and unhitched one of the poles from the side of the boat. As he reached for the other one, a boat's engine whined across the water.

He lifted his head in time to see a large powerboat cruise straight toward him. Maybe he was poaching on some locals' fishing territory.

That benign notion didn't last long when the boat drew closer, and three men in dark suits lined up along the starboard.

And they all had guns pointing straight at him.

Chapter Eight

Confronted with her son's scowling face, Tori tripped to a stop. Was the anger directed toward her? Did he already know who she was…and didn't like it?

Time to take control of her relationship with her son. To hell with allowing Alexi to call the shots.

Placing her hands on her hips, Tori tilted her head. "Why the unhappy face?"

Max wrinkled his nose and then punched a fist into the towering Legos. "I can't build my space station right and stupid Irina won't help me."

Tori gasped and shot a glance at Irina, who shrugged and returned to her book. Tori didn't want to spend precious time with Max disciplining him, but she didn't want any son of hers to be a brat.

"I'll be in the hallway." Ivan opened the door with a smirk and clicked it closed behind him.

Tori clenched her jaw. Time to be a mom. "Maksim Zherkov, you apologize to Irina right now."

Max spun around on his bottom, his mouth hanging open. "Who are you?"

Tori gulped. The SOB hadn't even told Max about her visit and had obviously forbidden Irina from doing so. As much as she wanted to curry favor with her son and make him like her, she was still his mother…and the sooner he figured that out, the better.

She dragged in a deep breath. "Max, I'm your mother, and you just said a very rude thing to Irina. You need to apologize to her. Now."

His green eyes widened and he dropped the Legos. He blinked a few times and then turned to Irina. "Sorry, Irina."

Irina eked out a tight smile. "I accept your apology, Maksim."

Max slid his gaze back to Tori. She held her breath. His eyes dropped to her feet, and he lowered his lashes. "I—I've never had a mom before."

Tori swallowed the lump in her throat and crossed the room. She crouched beside Max, resting her hand lightly on his back. "That's not true, Max. You've always had a mom. I haven't been able to be with you lately, but I always carry you right here in my heart."

He raised his gaze to her fist clenched against her chest. One corner of his mouth quirked upward. "Max. Nobody calls me Max…anymore."

"See, you do remember." She rubbed a circle on his stiff back. "I'm the only one who ever called you Max."

Max folded his legs beneath him and hunched forward, scooping up a Lego in his hand. "Can you build a spaceship?"

"Sure." Tori let out a long sigh between trembling lips. It was a start. At least he hadn't screamed and thrown Legos at her.

She dropped to the floor and crossed her legs. Patting her knees, she recited, "Crisscross applesauce."

Max giggled and crossed his legs, imitating her. He

snatched several Legos from the floor and threw them against the wall. "Stupid Legos."

Tori sucked in her lower lip. Alexi had been teaching by example, probably encouraging Max in his bad behavior and reminding him every five minutes of his status in Glazkova. Could she unravel two years of bad parenting in two weeks, or however long she had?

Oh, no. She didn't plan on giving up so easily this time. She ruffled Max's curly red hair with her fingers.

"Go pick up those Legos, Max, and we'll start from the beginning."

His lower lip jutted forward as he aimed an imperious green stare her way, but he wasn't a prince yet. He was just a little boy.

Her little boy.

"Go pick up those blocks. Then you can sit crisscross applesauce again and I'll help you with your spaceship." She turned away from him and began sorting the Lego pieces by size.

Max watched her for a moment, hunched his shoulders and scooted toward the scattered blocks. He shoved them toward her and scrambled back into his position next to her, crossing his legs beneath him and patting his knees.

They worked on the spaceship, exchanging few comments, but Max would slip a curious glance her way now and then. He remembered she called him Max. What else did he remember? Did he remember the love? The fun? The giggles? The crush of her hug the last time she saw him before she left Glazkova?

"It's time for your nap, Maksim." Irina snapped her book shut and placed it on the table beside her.

"I'm not a baby." Max jumped to his feet, clenching

small fists at his side. "I'm not going to take a baby nap. You don't think I'm a baby, do you?"

His freckles merged with his flushed face and a single curl hung in his eyes. Tori dug her nails into her thighs to keep from folding him in her arms. That wouldn't work with Max, not now.

She rose from the floor. As much as she wanted to keep Max with her every waking moment, she said, "I think you need to follow Irina's instructions and stay on your schedule. I'll be here when you wake up from your nap, Max."

Max's nostrils flared and then he kicked out at the spaceship on the floor. "No, you won't. I never had a mom 'cuz you left."

He charged toward the door and shoved it open, nearly smacking Ivan in the head.

Irina touched her arm. "Don't worry, Princess Victoria."

Tori twisted her lips into a smile, blinking back her tears. Max was right. She'd left him before, and she'd leave him again.

Ivan smirked as Irina brushed past him and then stepped into the room. "Someone got your stuff from the hotel. Do you want me to take you to your room now?"

"No." Tori squared her shoulders. "I want to stay here, alone, for a few minutes and look through my son's things. Close the door on your way out."

"I'll be in the hallway."

She shrugged. "Knock yourself out."

When Ivan closed the door, Tori turned and wandered around the well-appointed room. Alexi had given Max everything a four-year-old boy could ever want—toys, games, stuffed animals, his own flat-screen TV with a gaming system and piles of video games and DVDs.

She picked up one of the games, taking in the guns and blood on the cover. She tossed it back on the stack. "Totally inappropriate for a four-year-old."

The room contained none of the toys or books Tori had sent Max over the years. Had Alexi even given those gifts to Max? Probably not. He'd told Max that his mother had abandoned him. And hadn't she? She could've lived her days out in that palatial prison in Glazkova if she could be with her son.

No. Alexi would've found a way to turn Max against her. She had to get him away from his father. And Rio McClintock represented her best hope yet.

Which meant she'd better get busy and start digging up dirt on Alexi and his organization. Once she turned over the goods on Alexi, Rio would have to help her rescue Max.

A breeze rustled the drapes at the sliding glass door, open a crack. Tori shoved the drapes aside and slid open the door. As she stepped onto the balcony, a moist trade wind lifted strands of her hair, and a red ball rolled across the tile.

She leaned against the balcony's railing and gazed across the protected bay below. Her heart pounded as she spotted a fishing boat bobbing on the water. A single fisherman, shirtless, dark hair. Could it be?

Squinting against the sun, low on the horizon, she shaded her eyes. If only she had binoculars. The man seemed to be staring in her direction. It had to be Rio. He'd followed her. Wanted to make sure of her safety.

Voices in the hallway ratcheted up her already-racing heart. She glanced over her shoulder and then raised her arm toward the boat. The door burst open, and Tori dropped her arm abruptly.

Ivan stalked into the room and shouted, "Are you on the balcony?"

Ivan didn't need to see a boat outside Alexi's compound. He'd call out the dogs, and they'd be all over Rio. She slipped back inside and shut the sliding door behind her. "Just enjoying the view."

"Prince Alexi doesn't want you in here by yourself." He jerked his thumb over his shoulder. "I'll take you to your room."

As Tori followed Ivan out of the room, she cast a longing look back at the balcony.

I'm here, Rio. I'm safe. And I'm waiting for you.

RIO HELD UP HIS HANDS. "Whoa, dudes. Is this someone's private fishing hole or something? And what's with the suits?"

The man in the middle of the lineup waved his gun. "What are you doing here?"

The hot Maui sun blazed against Rio's bare back and a bead of sweat ran down his spine. He hoped Tori had gotten off that balcony. He raised his shoulders. "Just fishing, man. What's the problem?"

The man pointed to Alexi's mansion hugging the hillside. "You see that house?"

Rio nodded.

"My boss is renting that house, and he paid a lot to get some privacy." He swept his arm across the bay. "You're not allowed in this section of the ocean."

"Really? 'Cuz last time I checked, this was a free country."

The man spoke to one of his armed cohorts in Russian. Too bad for him he didn't know Rio spoke the language. He'd ordered the man to draw their boat closer to his, and Rio knew what that meant. Good thing he'd left his gun at the hotel, or this bunch would be wondering why an American fishing on vacation needed to pack a weapon.

"This may be a free country, but my boss paid well to secure this bay—call it capitalism at work."

Their powerful boat nudged Rio's smaller one, and two men hopped onto his deck. "Hey, what are you doing?"

"Shut up." One of the men smacked him on the back, pushing him forward.

Rio clenched his jaw, trying to keep a lid on his fury. A typical American tourist wouldn't try to take out four guys with guns. He had to play his role…for now.

While one thug held him at gunpoint, the other patted him down and then dumped out the contents of his pack. He grabbed the strap of the binoculars and held them up to the leader on the other boat.

"What are you doing with those?"

Rio scowled as he straightened up, pushing the hair from his eyes. "Scoping out the dolphins. Isn't this illegal or something?"

Alexi's gofer had relaxed his grip on his gun as the other man pawed through the seemingly innocent items in Rio's backpack. "I told you. My boss paid for a certain level of security. Law enforcement here on Maui is okay with our patrolling the bay."

Rio doubted that. "And I told you. I'm here to fish. If you want me to fish someplace else, just tell me."

"We want you to fish someplace else." The leader adjusted his sunglasses and lowered his weapon.

The man searching his belongings shoved the items into the pack and clutched the binoculars to his chest as he jumped onto his own boat. The other man, who'd kept Rio at gunpoint during the entire exchange, scrambled onto the other boat, too.

"Hey, what about my binoculars?"

The man holding the binoculars swung them over his head and let them fly. They splashed several feet away in the water, sinking quickly.

Rio cursed, playing the outraged tourist. "Why'd you do that?"

"Get out of this bay and don't come back."

Rio yanked the throttle on his rental boat and aimed toward the point jutting out at the edge of the bay. The black-suited goons followed him until he turned the corner and chugged toward the harbor.

Clenching his jaw, Rio narrowed his eyes. *I'll come back, all right. And when I do, there's gonna be hell to pay.*

Tori sank next to Max's bed and touched his soft cheek with her fingertip. She inhaled his scent—less baby and more little boy now, but still pure sweetness and innocence.

She leaned in close and touched her lips to the delicate curve of his ear. "I'm going to get you out of here, Max. We're going to get you out of here."

He stirred and mumbled in his sleep, swiping a hand across his eyes. Rolling onto his side, his lashes fluttered before he peeled open one eye.

"Hello," Tori whispered. "I'm still here."

Max rubbed his nose and struggled to sit up in his bed. "Did I break the spaceship?"

"Is that what you're worried about?" She flicked a curl from his forehead and snapped her fingers. "We can rebuild that in a flash."

The door to Max's bedroom squeaked, and he shifted his gaze over her shoulder. His green eyes clouded, and Tori knew without looking that her shadow, Ivan, had come into the room. Did his father's vigilance upset Max or did he accept it as normal? No child should have to view this imprisonment as typical.

Tori ignored Ivan's presence. "So what do you do after your nap? It's a little early for dinner, but would you like a snack?"

Max rubbed his eyes and nodded as a light rap sounded on the open door. This time Tori turned around.

Irina hovered at the threshold. "Why don't you have a snack, Max, and then you can show your mother how you're learning to ride a two-wheeler."

Your mother. Those two little words brought an ache to Tori's throat. She'd better control her tears, or Max would think she was a regular crybaby. She sucked in her breath and held it, wondering if Max would reject those words just as she treasured them.

He blinked his eyes a few times, and a shy smile inched across his face. "I don't need training wheels anymore."

That smile chipped away at the hard core of guilt in her belly. She might still need training wheels as a mom, but right now she was coasting.

After lots of mango and pineapple and a few spills on the drive in front of the estate, Max took a bath and they shared dinner together in the kitchen.

Then, with Ivan still hovering, Tori helped Max repair the Lego spaceship. When they'd fit the last piece into place, Irina poked her head in the door. "Time for bed, Max."

"Can I tuck you in?" Averting her face from Max, Tori

swept the remaining blocks into the bucket, desperate that Max not hear the longing in her voice.

"Okay." He hopped to his feet and extended his hand to her.

She'd risk anything and everything to have this sweetness in her life every day. And she'd have to deliver the goods to Rio to make him want to take the same risk.

She read a story to Max until his eyelids got heavy, and then she slipped out of his room. Ivan had disappeared at Max's bedtime, so maybe Alexi worried more about what she'd say to Max rather than the notion that she'd whisk him away.

Good. She needed her freedom in this house.

Tori scurried down the hallway and crouched at the balustrade at the top of the stairs. Irina had casually mentioned that Alexi planned to entertain guests tonight for dinner. The murmur of voices and the clink of fine crystal signaled their presence…and Alexi's preoccupation.

Once her bags had arrived from the hotel, Tori had showered and changed into a pair of capris and a blouse, but hadn't bothered with shoes. Now she crept silently down the stairs on bare feet and rounded the corner at the bottom.

She slipped into the library and clicked the door behind her. Anything Alexi had to hide, he'd keep in here—and he was a man of many secrets.

She tiptoed to the desk and tried the drawers. All locked. The screensaver on the computer flashed a series of pictures, and Tori shifted the mouse. She hissed with exasperation. Access to Alexi's computer required a password. She entered a few obvious guesses, but the cursor blinked back at her, refusing to open sesame.

She shuffled a few papers on Alexi's desk, but couldn't

read much from the light of the computer monitor. She should've thought to bring a little flashlight with her. She was ill-equipped to be a good spy.

Turning toward the bookshelf, she slipped out a volume of Russian poetry and leafed through the pages. Why had she been so sure she'd be able to get any info on Alexi? Although he trusted his underlings, he'd lock up anything incriminating.

Tori crossed her arms and surveyed the room, her eyes adjusting to the dark. She'd have to come up with a better method of obtaining information or at least get her hands on some proper tools of the trade for spying. Should've asked Rio about that, but then she'd had no idea Alexi's men would whisk her away before she had a chance to make plans with Rio.

Not that he'd wanted to make plans with her. Spying or otherwise. His rejection of her in the hotel room still stung. She must be losing her touch, or maybe she needed a good night's sleep.

She took a step toward the door, and then froze as the handle turned slowly. Low voices murmured outside in the hall as Tori spun around looking for cover. The heavy drapes were still drawn across the windows, so she dove into their folds, yanking them around her body.

She curled her toes away from the bottom edge of the drapes just as the library door swung open and her ex-husband whispered, "We can have some privacy in here."

Chapter Nine

Tori held her breath as the thick carpet muffled two sets of footsteps into the room. Someone clicked on the desk lamp and a yellow light glowed through the drapes.

A body moved behind the desk, the leather chair squeaking as it accepted his weight. Tori's nose twitched at the musky scent of Alexi's cologne. If she sneezed now, it would be all over.

"Do you trust this man, Vlad?" Alexi's fingers drummed on the desk. Must be nervous.

Vlad, the white-haired man she'd seen earlier, cleared his throat. "I've worked with him before. The deal went off smoothly enough."

"He enjoys his liquor and doesn't hold it well." The drumming stopped and Tori could imagine Alexi's eyes narrowed in a cold stare.

Vlad clicked his tongue. "Grant is young. He has a thing for the ladies, especially the ones who attend your parties, but business is business and Grant is serious about his business."

Alexi shifted in his chair. "Should we invite him in?"

Tori covered her mouth with her hand. She didn't need another person crowding into this room while she huddled behind the drapes, but this entire conversation sounded promising. Just the kind of info Rio might want.

"Don't sully your hands, Prince Alexi. That's why I'm here. Let me function as the go-between, and let Grant indulge in all the delights of your hospitality tonight."

Alexi smacked his hands on the desk and Tori started. "You are invaluable, Vlad. Does Grant want to sample the product before buying?"

"Not necessary. He trusts you, Alexi. This house, your parties…Grant feels as if the two of you are friends. He'll naturally have a little taste at the time of the exchange."

"Which is?"

Tori clenched her hands into fists, her nails digging into her palms. *Please don't write the time of the exchange on a piece of paper, Vlad.*

"Grant needs two more days to get the rest of the money. He wants a meeting on Thursday at nine o'clock."

Where, Vlad, where?

Alexi shoved back from the desk, his chair almost bumping Tori's knee. "At the location we discussed?"

"Yes."

"Excellent."

Tori would call this anything but excellent. She needed the location. She couldn't give Rio a date and a time without a place—somewhere in Maui wouldn't cut it.

The door snapped closed behind the men, and Tori sagged against the window, cooling her warm cheek against the pane. She really couldn't complain. She knew the when and she'd figure out the where—as soon as she learned the identity of the mysterious Grant.

But first she needed to communicate with Rio, and she had the perfect method. She just hoped he was as smart as he looked.

RIO GLANCED UP FROM HIS book, or rather Tori's book, for the hundredth time that morning. One hundred must be his lucky number.

Tori noticed him immediately but didn't drop her jaw or trip even once. That woman had a mind made for espionage, and a body made for…espionage.

She gripped the hand of a little carbon copy of herself, a boy with red, curly hair and a sprinkling of freckles across his nose. He tugged for escape as soon as they hit the playground and launched into the sand when Tori released his hand. The kid looked like a holy terror… yep, a carbon copy of Mom.

Two shadows dogged Tori as she sauntered into the park after her son. An older woman with jet black hair streaked with silver lagged behind them, a book tucked under her arm, and a big, bald dude followed more closely. Must be one of Alexi's goons sent to make sure Tori didn't abscond with Max.

For good measure, Rio waved at a gaggle of kids on the monkey bars, pretending a couple belonged to him. Wouldn't want to give Tori's bodyguard, who'd plopped onto a bench with his newspaper, the wrong impression.

Tori pushed Max on the swings for a while, and then he tore off to the monkey bars. Smart girl, didn't miss a thing. While the kids raced across the bars, chasing each other, Tori wandered toward Rio's bench.

"I'm surprised to see you here." She pointed to the kids swinging like a bunch of orangutans.

Baldy didn't even look up from his paper.

Rio smiled and waved to the kids again, whose parents probably had him pegged as some park perv by now. "You mentioned this spot at the pool. Since you didn't call me, I figured you didn't have use of your cell, and short of smoke signals, this place seemed like the best bet."

"I had actually planned to leave you something under the aforementioned rock. Just didn't expect to see you in the flesh."

"In the flesh is much better, isn't it?"

She smirked and hooked her thumbs in the pockets of her shorts, but a rosy color swept across her cheeks. "How long have you been out here?"

"Long enough to have some of the parents questioning my motives. Are you okay?"

"I'm fine. Why wouldn't I be? I'm with my son for the first time in two years and he doesn't hate me."

"Told you so. So, does that mean you're content to wait until the CIA rounds up your ex before making a move to get Max back?"

"No way. Do you want to hear what I found out?"

Rio's gut clenched. So Tori *had* been snooping around the compound. That could only mean trouble. "You don't have to…"

She sliced her hand across the air between them and turned it into a gesture toward the kids. "I do. Alexi's planning a meeting on Thursday night at nine o'clock with a guy named Grant. Don't know the place and don't know what Grant looks like…yet. But he hangs around the compound, so I can find out and get you a description. In fact, Alexi's hosting another party tonight. When I have something, I'll leave it under that rock tomorrow."

"Maybe the kids can have a play date. I'll check with

my wife." Rio turned away from Tori and yelled at a bunch of anonymous kids. "Be careful."

Tori sucked in a sharp breath. "That would be great."

"Irina said Maksim wants that shaved ice now." The hulking bodyguard loomed behind Tori, casting a shadow across Rio's legs.

"Okay." Tori wiggled her fingers in a wave. "Maybe we'll see you here again. I'm not sure about that play date though."

The man studied Rio through narrowed eyes as if committing him to memory. Rio hoped he didn't plan to compare notes with the thugs patrolling the water fronting the compound. He couldn't be both a trespassing tourist and a local dad overseeing the kiddies at the park.

He let out a long, ragged breath as Tori scooped up her son, and the odd foursome left the playground and ambled toward the shaved ice place...the same place where he and Tori had shared their first sticky kiss.

Smacking his fist against the bench, Rio muttered a curse under his breath. He should've deepened his relationship with Tori that first night when he'd had the chance. Maybe he could've sweet-talked her out of putting herself in that man's clutches again.

His lips twisted. Protection didn't cover half the reasons why he regretted putting the brakes on their connection the other night. He wanted her—pure and simple, or maybe there was nothing pure about it.

Rio blew out a breath, teeming with frustration. Running into Tori had complicated his job. He pushed off the bench, his gaze tripping over the big rock under the tree. Thursday at nine o'clock with Grant.

Or maybe she'd made his job easier.

"WHO WAS THAT MAN YOU were talking to in the park?" Ivan's steely gaze drilled her to the core, making her shiver more than the ice melting on her tongue.

Tori slurped a spoonful of grape ice and lifted a shoulder. "Some dad in the park. Max was playing with his kids. I suppose Alexi doesn't arrange play dates."

"No. Maksim won't be here that long."

Leaning forward, Tori dabbed a napkin to Max's cherry mustache, controlling her trembling hand. "Did you have fun in the park?"

"Uh-huh. Can we go to the beach next?" Max ran the tip of his red tongue around his mouth.

"I think it's time for lunch and a nap. Maybe after your nap."

Storm clouds rolled across Max's face, and his chin jutted forward. "I don't like naps."

"I know that, but you don't want to be tired when we're at the beach, do you?"

Max raised his eyes to the sky as if contemplating the merits of naptime and came back smiling. "No. I won't be tired at the beach."

"Good. Let's go home."

As they passed the park, Tori's gaze darted around its perimeter. Rio had disappeared. She hadn't realized how tense she'd been at Alexi's compound until she'd seen Rio sitting on that bench. Even with Ivan in the vicinity, Tori had felt secure and reassured as soon as she'd heard Rio's voice.

A smile curved her lips as she recalled his waving to those puzzled kids. His dark dangerousness seemed at odds with the image of a concerned parent. He'd most likely be uneasy with kids, but he'd do anything to protect them. That's what she had to count on.

As they walked through the park on the way back to

the car, Tori threw one last glance at the innocuous rock under the tree. It looked inconspicuous now, but that hunk of obsidian represented Max's ticket to freedom.

RIO CREASED THE SCRAP of paper into a sharp edge and tapped it on the steering wheel of his rental car. He'd put in an afternoon of sleuthing, bribing and trailing, and his payoff just stumbled out of the No Ka Oi Bar and Lounge.

He slid from the car and adjusted his sunglasses. As his prey fumbled with the keys to his car, Rio silently sidled up next to him. "Do you want to make some quick cash, Jacob?"

Jacob dropped his keys and swayed on his feet, blinking at Rio as if he'd just conjured him from a drunken haze. "Huh? Do I know you?"

"We have a few mutual friends on the island." Yeah, like the woman Rio had paid off over an hour ago to meet up with Jacob in the bar and buy him a few too many drinks. "Word's out that you have a good gig tonight up at the compound at Haiku Bay."

Unable to stop his swaying, Jacob slumped against his car. "Yeah. What's it to you?"

Rio dug into the pocket of his shorts and pulled out a wad of cash. "I'd like to take your place."

Jacob eyed the money and belched. "Why?"

"Just trying to get next to a woman." Rio winked. He always tried to stay as close to the truth as possible.

"I dunno. The catering company's being hard-ass about this job, checking our names against a list."

"If the catering company's being hard-ass, they're not going to like it when you show up blitzed." Rio raised his brows. "I'll pay you double what the catering company is going to pay."

Jacob licked his lips. "Three times and you got a deal."

Rio agreed, and Jacob shoved the uniform for the evening into Rio's arms, plopping the black shoes on top of the pile. "I hope the chick is worth all the cash, man."

"Oh, yeah. She's worth it."

TORI STOOD AT THE WINDOW of one of the bedrooms facing the entrance of the house watching Alexi's guests arrive for the continuation of the festivities from the night before. Last night he'd hosted a dinner, but tonight was party time.

Max had acquiesced to his nap without much fuss, and when he had awakened, Tori had asked Ivan to drive them to a small protected beach with slow rolling waves. She realized part of Max's acceptance of her revolved around her willingness to take him out of the compound. She got the impression that Irina didn't go out much. But Tori didn't mind.

She'd do whatever it took to win her son back…short of bribery and bad parenting.

As Tori watched the pretty people file onto the estate, an idea that had been forming ever since she'd run into Rio in the park crystallized into resolution. What better way to give Rio a description of Grant than to meet him up close and personal?

Tori slipped out of the bedroom and crossed the hall-way to her own room. She'd already showered after the beach. Now she just had to fit in with the glittering crowd downstairs. Smiling, she threw open the closet doors; she knew there was a good reason why she never went anywhere without a little black dress.

She slid the dress off the hanger, its silky material

slipping through her hands. The dress whispered as she stepped into it and pulled the zipper up to her waist. She shrugged out of her bra and tied the halter-style neckline, leaving her back bare.

Digging through a suitcase in the corner of the closet, she dragged out a pair of black, high-heeled, strappy sandals. Maybe this getup couldn't compete with the designer duds and diamond doodads sported by the ladies downstairs, but it should be enough to get her one little conversation with Grant.

Tori played up her green eyes, trailing black eyeliner past the corners for a catlike effect. She kissed her glossed lips at her reflection in the mirror and growled. If Grant liked the ladies, she'd give him a lady to like.

Tori paced in her room for almost an hour, giving the guests more time to arrive to provide her cover. Alexi didn't seem to care whether or not she showed up at his social functions, but she didn't want her ex to notice her seeking out Grant.

When the buzz from the party reached a steady hum, Tori descended the staircase and snagged a flute of champagne from a roving waiter before entering the great room. She hadn't exercised her party skills in quite a while, but just like riding a bike, she'd be pedaling in no time.

Over the rim of her glass, Tori surveyed the scene. Grabbing a crab puff, she sidled up to a group babbling about casinos in Monaco. Soon the same froth bubbled from her own lips. After all, she'd been there, done that…in another life. She fit right in.

She introduced herself to the group as Tori—no last names required. She didn't need to make a scene as Alexi's ex-wife. She listened carefully to their first names. Since none of the men admitted to being a Grant, she wandered to the next group.

Alexi swooped into the room and spotted her immediately. Unfortunately, the man seemed to have radar where she was concerned. She gave a slight nod of her head and he returned the gesture, cutting a path through his guests.

"Are you enjoying yourself?" His gaze swept from her head to her toes in a split second.

"The crab puffs are good." She held the little delicacy aloft, waving it in front of his face.

His nose twitched. "You are being discreet as I requested, Victoria?"

"Discretion is my middle name." She popped the crab puff in her mouth and mumbled, "And Tori is my first."

"Excellent. Then have a good time and eat all the crab puffs you like." He straightened his cuffs and brushed past her.

Yeah, she'd do that, oh, and find Grant.

She exchanged inanities with a few more plastic people, none named Grant. Wandering onto the patio, she nearly tripped and fell into the bubbling hot tub, already crowded with slick bodies. Most of those bodies had curves, except for one man lounging against the side, one arm each draped across the shoulders of two bikini-clad babes. How had they shed their party clothes so quickly?

Tori dragged a chair close to the edge of the Jacuzzi and took a sip of champagne. A player would most likely hang out in the hot tub with the ladies. She'd been an expert on the species at one time.

Kicking her legs up on the chair across from hers,

Tori leaned back, pretending to stargaze, and listened in on what passed for conversation between these people. She needed to hear one name.

"Do you want to join us?"

Tori's gaze shifted to the grinning man in the hot tub. She batted her mascaraed lashes. "I didn't bring my bikini."

"No bikini necessary." He wiggled his eyebrows up and down. "I'm sure Alexi wouldn't mind."

She laughed. Although she had no intention of climbing into that hot tub, his smarmy invitation had given her the opportunity to ask his name. She opened her mouth and a tray of drinks appeared beneath her nose.

"Would you like another?"

The low voice sent a ripple of desire down to her toes. Slipping her legs from the chair, she sat up and grasped her glass. She raised her eyes to the bearded cocktail waiter hovering beside her, his tray loaded with champagne flutes balanced on his palm. He'd slicked back his long hair and gathered it into a short ponytail, but those chocolate brown eyes still burned with intensity, turning her insides to jelly.

No mistake about it—Rio McClintock was in the house.

THE LADY KEPT HER COOL. Her gaze darted around the patio, and then she frowned into her champagne flute. "Are you crazy?"

"Are you?" Hot tub boy had already lost interest in Tori and was passionately kissing one of the blondes who flanked him. Rio had interrupted just in time. No way would he allow Tori to slip out of the sexy number that hugged the curves of her body and hop into the Jacuzzi.

"Ivan has already seen you once today."

"Not with a beard, and I don't think Ivan was invited."

"He might not have been invited, but you can bet your false facial hair he's lurking around here somewhere. Alexi's guys do a lot of lurking."

"Yeah, I know. They harassed me on the water, too."

She gasped. "Then you really are crazy."

He lifted a glass from the tray and took her half-filled one. "Meet me in the kitchen."

Jerking her head toward the hot tub, she whispered, "But I think that might be our man. I was getting close."

"Too close. He *is* our man." Rio's too-small rubber-soled black shoes squished through the water pooling on the patio as he walked toward the hot tub. He crouched and extended the tray to Grant and his bevy of beauties. "More champagne?"

Grant grabbed two stems with his stubby fingers. "Who's ready for more?"

The women squealed and grabbed for the remaining glasses while Rio studied Grant. *He must be new to the game since he didn't warrant a blip on the CIA's radar.* Before he ran into Tori earlier today, Rio had already scoped out the known drug dealers on the island and none showed signs of a major deal going down.

The way Grant soaked up the high life had *novice* written all over it. Rio didn't need the location of the drop. He'd tail Grant like a dog sniffing meat.

The women emptied his tray, and Rio jostled through the crowd back to the kitchen. As he loaded up another tray, Tori staggered through the swinging doors.

"Hey, can a girl get some crab puffs around here?"

Tori slurred her words and grabbed the edge of the chrome island in the middle of the busy kitchen.

If any of the catering staff recognized her as the Prince's ex, they didn't blink an eye.

Rio parked his tray on the countertop and stooped down, cinching the handles of the nearest garbage bag. "I'm going to empty this out back. Any more trash to go out?"

"You can take this one." One of the staff kicked at a bulging bag and Rio plucked it up in his other hand.

As he kicked open the back door to the side of the house, Tori gagged.

"Uh-oh, I think I'm going to be sick." She rushed past him and out the door.

Rio smiled as he hoisted the trash bags. *Man, that woman had an endless well of resources.* He shut the kitchen door behind him and hauled the trash toward the bin at the corner of the house.

Tori stepped from the shadows. "How do you know that man is Grant?"

"Over there." Rio thrust his chin toward the shadows beyond the trash bin. She followed him into the darkness and he hoisted the plastic garbage bags into the bin.

Brushing his hands together, he turned toward Tori. The moon cast a shimmering glow around her red hair, and her green cat eyes made her look like some fire goddess from the volcano.

"I got here before you did, princess. I did a little covert recon around the property. When the party started, I lingered as I passed around the drinks and caught several names before I hit pay dirt."

"How'd you get in here, and if it was so easy how come you didn't do it before? I know Alexi's had plenty of parties here before this one."

Rio patted his fake goatee. He had a harder time answering that question. Sure, he could've infiltrated the catering staff on any number of occasions over the past few months he'd been watching Alexi. But he'd never wanted to take the risk…before. Once Tori had entered the picture, his tolerance for risk had climbed sky-high. He didn't want to leave her here on her own.

"Well?"

He lifted a shoulder. "Thanks to you, I had a purpose. You gave me a name, and I wanted to match it with a face."

"But I planned to give you that information. Don't you trust me?"

"I trust you, princess." He brushed a strand of hair from her cheek. "I don't trust Ivan. I couldn't know with certainty if you'd make it back to that park, or if you'd get the opportunity to leave me a note beneath the rock. Didn't want Ivan catching you in the act, putting you in harm's way."

"Now you've put yourself in harm's way." She shivered.

"Better me than you." He wedged his hands on the rough stucco on either side of Tori's shoulders. Her musky perfume invaded his senses, and each time her pulse throbbed in her throat, another warm wave of scent enveloped him.

Dipping his head, he kissed her mouth, tasting the fruity champagne on her lips. She gripped his forearms and kissed him back, hard and sweet.

The side kitchen door banged open and Tori jerked. Rio pressed his body along hers, and her heart beat wildly against his chest.

"Hey, dude. You still out here? I need help delivering booze to hot chicks."

Rio touched a finger to Tori's lips, still moist from the kiss. It wouldn't do for the other bartender, Hugo, to find him out back with one of the guests…the host's ex-wife and the hottest chick at the party.

One footstep hit the gravel, and then Hugo must've thought better of venturing any farther into the darkness. The kitchen door creaked and slammed shut.

Tori released a pent-up breath. "We'd better get out of here. If we're caught…"

"Was it worth it?" Rio traced a fingertip around her mouth.

"You had your chance, cowboy." She grabbed his hand. "You passed when we had a nice, safe hotel room. You prefer making out under the threat of danger?"

"Maybe it's the beard that's making me reckless."

She tugged at his fake facial hair. "You go through the kitchen and get back to work, and I'll wander down by the lawn and make my way into the house through the patio."

"Be careful."

Tori broke away from Rio's warm embrace and crept toward the torchlit path to the grassy lawn that rolled to the edge of the cliff. She glanced over her shoulder to find him still watching her from the shadows and pressed her fingers against her lips as if to keep his kiss there.

She kicked off her sandals and hooked her fingers around the straps. Her toes squished against the wet grass as she sauntered toward the cliff that tumbled into the ocean. Alexi didn't allow Max anywhere near this lawn without close supervision. His parenting skills definitely needed work, but at least he watched out for Max's physical safety.

She planned to walk along the edge and then cut through the patio. She didn't want anyone to make a connection between her and the handsome bartender with the black goatee.

Dance music from the party boomed across the yard. Alexi must've kicked things up a notch. The thumping beat ruined the beauty and solitude of the scene spread before her.

Tori stepped out of the edge of light cast by the house and gazed across the ocean. A soft breeze toyed with the hem of her dress and she inhaled the fragrant air. Maybe if the CIA nailed Alexi on this drug deal, she could scoop up Max and make a quick getaway.

A muffled thud and a groan filtered through the thick foliage bordering the lawn to her right. Tilting her head, Tori crept toward the bushes and parted the branches and leaves.

Two men struggled near the edge of the cliff. Shouting, Tori scrambled through the foliage and landed on her knees, the dirt and sand on the other side of the bushes pressing into her flesh.

Both men looked up. The darkness obscured their features, but one had a beard and the white shirt of the caterers. Tori launched to her feet and yelled, "Hey! What are you doing out here?"

The bearded man choked out a response, which the other man's fist cut off. The waiter stumbled backward, his arms flailing to his sides. His attacker shoved the teetering form off the edge of the cliff.

The bearded man disappeared into thin air without even uttering a cry.

Blood pounded against Tori's temples, and the metallic taste of fear flooded her mouth. She spun around toward the bushes and slipped, grunting as she landed on the rough ground. Heavy footsteps crunched the dirt behind her and a calloused hand clamped across her mouth.

A voice growled in her ear. "Don't tell anyone about this accident, princess, or you'll never see your son again."

Chapter Ten

The hand pressed against her mouth shifted to the back of her head, blunt fingers plowing through her hair. Her assailant tipped her forward and shoved her face into the dirt.

He growled, "Stay there."

Panting, Tori inhaled bits of sand, her muscles tense and aching. The man gave her one more push before heaving to his feet and plowing through the bushes.

Tori scrambled to her hands and knees and crawled toward the cliff's edge. Sobs wracked her chest as she peered down at the swirling water. The tiny slice of moon didn't do much to illuminate the scene, but either the water swept the man away or he lay sprawled on the jagged rocks. Nobody could survive that fall...not even Rio McClintock.

She screamed into the abyss, "Rio!"

Staggering to her feet, she brushed the dirt from her knees and ran her hands across her face. There was only one way to discover if Rio had been the bearded man in the fight.

She retrieved her sandals by the bushes and smoothed her dress. Ducking, she picked her way through the foliage and almost ran across the lawn to the patio.

While she brushed the wet grass from her feet, she

studied the partygoers lounging in the hot tub or sharing intimate conversations in the shadows of the house. Nobody had heard the drama on the cliff.

A waiter bearing a tray of drinks and appetizers floated onto the patio, and Tori's gut twisted. Not Rio. He didn't float.

She slid into the house, her gaze darting around the room lighting on one white-jacketed man after another, the sick feeling in her stomach rising with each disappointment.

Her heart stopped. Rio exited the kitchen, his long hair tucked up under a cap. When his gaze collided with hers, he raised his brows. Tori glanced around the room quickly, and then tilted her chin back toward the kitchen. She had to speak to him again, and that secluded spot behind the trash bin seemed like a good bet.

Rio continued his rounds of the room, tray in hand, and Tori wandered back toward the patio, flirting along the way just like any other guest enjoying the party. She exchanged banter with a couple near the Jacuzzi, and then slipped into the yard. She crept up to the corner of the house and peeked around it.

The kitchen door burst open. "Any more trash to go out?"

Rio's insistence on hauling trash probably made him the most popular member of the catering staff. He trudged toward her, two plastic garbage bags clenched in each hand.

He dropped one into the bin. "We can't keep meeting like this. It's dangerous. Have you noticed? All of a sudden Alexi's goons have made an appearance at the party."

Her mouth almost too dry to speak, Tori ran her

tongue along her teeth. "You have to get out of here, Rio. Now."

Jerking his head up, he narrowed his eyes. "Why?"

"I—I just witnessed a murder."

"What?"

"One of Alexi's men pushed another man from the cliff. I saw it all. I thought it was you. The killer then threatened me." She choked and dug the heels of her hands into her eyes.

Rio's strong arms went around her, drawing her against his chest. "Could it have been two of Alexi's guys going at it?"

"No." She sniffled against his shirt, inhaling his warm, masculine scent. She wanted to stay right here, but Rio had to leave. Gathering his shirt in her hands she looked into his face. "I thought it was you because the man was dressed in a white shirt and black pants... and he had longish hair and a beard."

Rio sucked in his breath. "Hugo. We have to call the police."

"No!" Tori yanked at his shirt. "We can't do that. The man who killed Hugo told me that if I told anyone, I'd never see Max again. He means it, Rio. If I cause any trouble for Alexi here, he'll snatch Max away from me."

"Is there any chance he could've survived the fall?"

"No. You should know that cliff face better than anyone. If the rocks on the way down didn't kill him, the water did. The ocean on this side of the island is rough in the winter. I looked over the edge, but I couldn't see or hear anything. Hugo's gone, Rio, and now you have to leave. Alexi knows something."

Rio scratched at his fake beard. "That's why I put this cap on and tucked in my hair. When the goon squad showed up en masse I figured something was up. The guy I paid off to take his position must've spilled his guts, but why go after Hugo?"

"How long before they question the next waiter with a beard and long hair?" She pushed against his broad chest. "Get out."

"Come with me. I don't want to abandon you here alone." He grabbed her hand.

"No." She yanked out of his grasp. "I can't leave Max. I won't leave Max again."

"What if Alexi hurts you because you witnessed the murder?"

"Even if Alexi's thug tells him about it, Alexi won't harm me. He'll just use it against me. He has Max. He knows I'll do anything to see him. But my guess is Alexi's guy isn't going to be too anxious to tell his boss that he killed someone while his ex-wife watched."

Rio took her face in his hands. He brushed the pad of his thumb across her mouth, and then replaced it with his lips. Tori sagged against his body, getting lost in the desire that washed across her skin.

He whispered against her hair. "I want you out of here, Tori."

Tracing her fingertip along the hard ridge of his jaw, she kissed the muscle ticking there. "Then disrupt Alexi's deal with Grant."

THE FOLLOWING DAY TORI folded her arms across her stomach as she joined the clutch of staff members peering over the drop-off. Had someone found Hugo's body already?

"What are you looking at?" She sidled up next to Alexi's personal chef.

He pointed to a rainbow-hued parachute. "Someone's parasailing."

Relaxing her shoulders, Tori blew out a breath. Someone parasailing beat out a dead body any day. As she turned to leave, one of the security guards caught her arm.

"Prince Alexi would like to see you in his library."

The tension she'd just released gripped her shoulders again, but she pasted on a smile. "Lucky me."

What did Alexi want with her? He must know something. Had the killer from last night really admitted to Alexi that Tori had been present when Hugo went over the side? Did they realize yet that they killed the wrong guy, that Hugo had represented no threat to them?

Tori wiped her palms against her cotton skirt before tapping on the library door. Alexi called out, "Enter."

She pushed at the heavy door and paused on the threshold. Alexi glanced up impatiently from his papers and snapped his fingers. "Come in and shut the door behind you."

"What do you want, Alexi? I'm not one of your gofers you can summon at will by snapping your fingers." She slammed the door behind her. Tough talk always gave her strength.

And a poker face would keep her alive.

He looked up, a slow smile spreading across his face. Yeah, she knew why she'd fallen for him—dark, dangerous and silky smooth. She'd always gone for the dark and dangerous type, but while sharp sophistication marked Alexi, rough masculinity defined Rio. She'd put her money on rough and masculine any day.

"That's what attracted me to you, Victoria. You always had fire, especially in bed."

She widened her eyes. "You mean even when I was drugged?"

He laughed. "Lust was our drug."

"Crack must be your drug now if you believe that." She wedged a shoulder on the doorjamb. "Besides, I thought you were attracted to me because of that green-eyed, red-haired lucky charm thing I had going."

His nostrils flared as he dropped a sheaf of papers on his desk, a dull red staining his cheeks. His superstitious nature embarrassed him, but not enough to abandon it. "That, too."

"Did you call me in here to discuss my…fire?"

"Did you enjoy yourself last night, Victoria?" Alexi rested his elbows on the table, his dark eyes now flat and unreadable.

"Sure. Good food, good drink and vacuous company. What's not to like?"

"You used to enjoy vacuous people. You felt right at home with them."

Tori winced and then ground her teeth. He had her there. She'd been as shallow as the rest of them, trying hard to distance herself from her staid, religious family and then later to bury the guilt over her parents' deaths beneath a round of parties.

"Then I had a son." She shrugged off the doorjamb and straightened her spine.

"Ah, yes, Maksim."

"Get to the point, Alexi."

He shoved up from his chair, his tall, lean form hunching over the desk as he flattened his hands on the surface. "I'm taking Maksim home next week."

His words punched her in the gut and she swayed on her feet. "But you said…"

Alexi sliced his hand through the air. "I said you

could visit with him here for as long as we stayed. We're leaving."

Tori's thoughts ricocheted through her brain at warp speed. If the CIA moved in on Alexi tonight, could they bring him in immediately? If she notified Rio that Alexi planned to leave next week, could he speed up the process? "You can't leave."

Alexi straightened to his full height and slammed his fist against the desktop. "I can do whatever I wish. I'm Prince Alexi of Glazkova."

"I'll get an attorney. Hell, I'll call in a whole battery of attorneys. I'll tie you up in so many legal knots you won't be able to make a move without consulting the courts."

Cold steel shot through his voice. "Don't threaten me, Victoria. I can whisk Maksim out of this country at a moment's notice."

She squeezed her eyes shut against the hot tears burning behind her lids. She wouldn't allow herself to break down in front of this man.

"We don't need to battle." He stepped from behind the desk and leaned his hip on the corner. "I have a proposition for you that will allow you to spend Christmas with Maksim. You'd like that, wouldn't you?"

Wiping her nose with the back of her hand, she raised her chin. "What kind of proposition?"

"Come home with us."

Tori staggered back, bashing her thigh against a bookshelf. "T-to Glazkova?"

"I can make all the unpleasantness of your charges go away." He spread his hands, which looked soft and effeminate compared to Rio's. "Come back with me as my wife, as Maksim's mother, the rightful Princess of Glazkova."

"I can't do that. You're a criminal. You exploit people's weaknesses and make money off of them."

He shrugged. "What do you care of that? My mother never meddled in my father's business. Turn a blind eye. Enjoy all that Glazkova has to offer the royal family, enjoy your son."

"And if I displease you in some way? You'll take Max away or trump up some phony charges against me."

"Don't displease me."

A shiver ran through her body. Hugging herself, Tori turned away from Alexi's piercing gaze. What if she pretended to accept his offer? Right here. Right now. Her chances of escaping with Max might be better.

She had to play this right. She couldn't acquiesce too easily. Time to take advantage of those acting classes she'd dabbled in when she'd lived in L.A.

Biting her lip, she glanced over her shoulder. "I'd be with Max? You wouldn't interfere with our relationship?"

"Maksim needs a mother. I see that now."

"And you'd conduct your business outside of the palace? I don't want Max's life endangered by the shady characters that comprise your business associates. I don't want to see evidence of it in our home."

"I've already done that." He brushed his hands together. "I have a secure center of operations now. Nothing is conducted out of the palace anymore."

She clasped her hands in front of her, turning slowly. "And you promise I'll get to be with Max as much as I like?"

"He's your son." He extended his hand. "Come. Let's seal this deal with a kiss."

Her flesh crawled with disgust. If she gave in too easily, he might suspect her. If she didn't give in at all, he might withdraw the offer. She took a shaky step forward. "Th-this might be too soon, Alexi. I'm just getting used to this idea. I haven't committed myself to it yet."

He raised one dark brow. "I realize there's a lot of animosity between us. You betrayed me, and I took Maksim away from you. But I'm offering you a chance to be with him again. Let's take this first step."

She shifted her gaze from his face to his proffered hand and back again. Licking her lips, she edged closer. His familiar cologne almost made her gag.

Just as she scooped in a deep breath, his arm shot out and wrapped around her waist. He dragged her into his sphere and pressed his heated lips against hers.

Instinctively, she jerked back, but his fingers weaved through her hair and he pulled her closer, parting her lips with his tongue.

The library door swung open and they jumped apart.

Alexi's right-hand man and accountant, Melvin, colored to the roots of his hair. "I'm so sorry, Prince Alexi. I knocked and thought I heard a response."

Alexi rounded on him and snapped, "What is it?"

The man cleared his throat as two uniformed officers stepped into the room behind him. "There are two policemen here, Prince Alexi. They have questions about one of the catering staff from last night."

"Questions? What kind of questions?"

One of the officers stepped around Melvin and flipped open a notebook. "The body of one of the waiters from your party last night washed up on a beach a few miles north of here."

Alexi shrugged, his face a mask. "That's unfortunate, but what does that have to do with me? There were no accidents here last night."

Tori folded her hands in front of her, trying not to wipe Alexi's disgusting kiss from her mouth.

The officer scribbled something in his notebook. "Your party is the last place he was seen alive. Did any of your guests report anything unusual last night? Anyone staggering along the cliff edge? The young man had a large quantity of alcohol in his system."

"I'm sorry, officer. My guests enjoyed the party and then left. The caterer did not report anyone missing."

After a few more questions, which Alexi stonewalled, the officer snapped his notebook shut and pocketed it. "I suggest you find another caterer to use, Mr. Zherkov, one that more carefully screens its employees. The victim, Hugo Holloway, was a small-time drug dealer and big-time user."

Tori bit the inside of her cheek. Could Hugo's murder have been unrelated to Rio's infiltration of the catering staff? Tori checked her watch. Six more hours to go before the nine o'clock meeting. With Alexi packing up Max to send him home next week, Rio had to pull this off tonight.

As the officers left the library, Tori followed in their wake.

Alexi laid a hand on her shoulder. "We're not done here, Victoria. In fact, I have a second proposition for you."

Slipping from his hold, she aimed a shaky smile over her shoulder. "It's time for Max to wake up from his nap. I'll come back later."

Alexi's lips tightened, but he nodded and stepped back, gesturing to Melvin to follow him back to his desk.

Tori sighed as she snapped the library door shut. She took the stairs two at a time, putting as much distance between herself and Alexi as quickly as possible. Another kiss from her ex-husband and she'd hurl her delicious lunch.

Only one man could claim her kisses.

AT 8:23 THAT EVENING, Rio narrowed his eyes as he slumped in the seat of the rental car and pulled the cap low over his forehead. Two men exited the Escalade and slipped through the gate to Grant's house. Game time.

Rio clicked open his car door and hunched forward. Grasping the tracking device in his hand, he hurried across the street to the rear of the car. He ducked beneath the chassis and smacked the device against the inside of the tire well. He crawled on his belly back to his own car and slid inside.

Grant Swain. He hadn't been too hard to track— ambitious drug dealer on the move to the big leagues. The CIA already had him on its radar, and Rio's information had just turned him into a big blip on that radar. Tori's information.

Rio had faced one of the hardest decisions of his life last night, leaving Tori in that nest of vipers. But it wasn't his decision to make. Now that she had Max back in her arms, she'd never leave her son. Rio had seen it in her eyes, a fierce light of protective motherhood.

Something he'd never seen in his own mother's eyes.

And what if Alexi escaped with Max? Would Tori follow him back to Glazkova? Risk her own life to be with her son? Rio clenched his teeth as hard as he clenched the steering wheel of the car. He knew the answer to that. But he'd never allow it.

He rubbed his jaw and took a sip of lukewarm Kona coffee. He'd been following Swain all day, and the man obviously anticipated a big score. He'd been on a shopping spree with not one, but two of the lovely ladies from the hot tub last night.

Even if the CIA didn't plan to put a crimp in Swain's career trajectory tonight, the guy wouldn't have lasted long in this business. A successful drug dealer, one in it for the long haul, had to have cold, calculated viciousness on his side. Kind of like Mad Prince Alexi.

Minutes later, the two men, with Swain in the lead, strode from the house and jumped into the Escalade. Rio released a long breath. He had figured Swain wouldn't take his own car. He tilted the collar of his shirt toward his chin. "Target tagged and on the move, heading north."

"Roger that," Jake Burns, the CIA's leader on this task force, responded.

Rio waited until the Escalade turned the corner before starting his engine and pulling forward. Two agents up ahead would pick up Swain's trail, and if they happened to lose him or if they couldn't follow him to a deserted location for fear of being spotted, they'd catch up with him later. Rio patted the GPS device on the passenger seat, now following the Escalade's every twist and turn.

After twenty minutes on Maui's main highway, Swain pulled off on the road toward Hana. They couldn't chance following him past the last town on the rough, inhospitable road.

Rio's earpiece crackled and Burns's voice sounded loud and clear. "We're pulling off in Paia. Is that GPS working?"

Rio glanced at the screen. "Yep. The little red dot is moving through Paia as we speak. Is the helicopter ready?"

"Just as soon as you tell us when and where that fish lands."

Rio pulled into town and swung off the main drag, parking in front of a T-shirt store. The dot representing the Escalade bleeped and blinked along a path heading away from the ocean. Then it stopped. Rio noted the location and coordinates and relayed them to the team of anxious CIA agents waiting in the wings. He knew his words had just sent them scrambling into action.

He grabbed the GPS and his gun, abandoning his little rental car. He zigzagged through some back streets until he spotted Burns's Jeep and vaulted into the cramped backseat.

Burns gunned the engine. "Let's do this."

They were going in with eight agents in three cars, with Rio along for the ride and four more agents in the helicopter. Rio didn't know how many men Alexi would send, but if Swain had just two others beside himself, they'd disrupt this little party easily enough.

They'd link Alexi's men to him, and that should be good enough for an arrest. Maybe Tori would have enough time to take Max away. Rio would do his best to make it happen that way.

They pulled the Jeeps off the road and began the hike to the drop location on foot. They'd call in the chopper once they secured the location and disarmed the men.

The Escalade and one other car had pulled up to a small house. Rio rolled his shoulders. Alexi couldn't have sent too many men in one car. This should go smoothly, thanks to Tori.

Rio crept up to the house, gun drawn. Blinds covered the windows, but a steady light glowed inside. Rio, Burns and another agent, Ted Phillips, took the front, while two agents had the backdoor and the other two took up positions on either side of the house to watch the windows. The remaining two agents waited by the road.

Burns contacted the chopper and then held his hand out toward Rio while he leaned in close to the door. A hum of voices carried through the front door. Rio's muscles coiled, ready to spring on Burns's command.

Suddenly, the voices inside rose to shouts. Burns and Rio exchanged a glance. The same thought must've crossed Burns's mind as Rio's—take advantage of the situation inside. Burns gave the order to move.

Rio and Burns kicked in the front door, while the two agents in the back crashed through the rear. Chaos erupted. A few of the men in the room scrambled for the windows, but an announcement from the chopper stopped them cold.

Burns shouted, "Place your weapons on the floor and put your hands against the walls. All of you."

The agents streamed into the room, collecting weapons and handcuffing men before pushing them to the floor. Swain stood in the middle of the room, arms held high. "We didn't do anything. We don't have anything."

"Shut up." Burns grabbed him by the back of the neck and shoved him against the wall.

Rio grabbed the edge of a duffel bag on the floor and peeled it back. Rows of neatly stacked cash lined the bag. His gaze shifted to the bags in the other corner of the room. Alexi's drugs—probably heroin culled from the poppy fields of Afghanistan where he still had connections.

One of the agents snorted. "Hey, Mad Prince Alexi has a chick working for him."

Rio glanced in the direction of the agent's voice. The agent had his hand between the suspect's legs, and then he reached up and pulled off the black knit cap.

The room reeled beneath Rio's feet as the suspect's hair tumbled around her shoulders.

The agent growled, "On the floor, sister, with the rest of your comrades."

The woman turned and her back slid down the wall until she landed in a puddle on the floor. She brushed her red hair out of her face and raised her green eyes to Rio's. Choking, she reached out a hand to him.

"Hey, don't try anything, sister." The agent smacked the side of her head with the butt of his gun.

And Tori slumped into a heap.

Chapter Eleven

Rage burned through Rio's veins, and he lurched toward the agent looming over Tori. He bunched his fists, ready to take the man's head off, until Tori shot him a warning glance before squeezing her eyes closed in obvious pain.

He flexed his fingers and put a hand out toward the pumped up agent. "Hold on. I don't know about you, but I'm old school and we don't treat women harshly even if they are the scum of the earth."

The man flushed as he lifted a shoulder. "I thought she might be going for a weapon."

Rio crouched in front of Tori, dressed all in black, and asked gruffly, "You okay?"

She righted herself awkwardly with her hands cuffed behind her and smirked. "I'll be okay as soon as you give me that guy's name so I can report him for brutality."

The agent huffed behind Rio. "See? You're wasting your time. This one's no lady."

"Maybe not." Rio pushed up, wondering how in the hell Tori had gotten involved in this mess. "But we'd better have a female agent or officer at the police station when we book her to do a full body search, or we will be in trouble."

A commotion across the room drew Rio's attention.

A couple of agents pawed through the bags in the corner while Burns hovered over them and Swain screamed obscenities at Alexi's men and Tori, lined up against the wall.

Burns shoved Swain out of the way and stomped across the room toward Rio. "We have a problem, McClintock."

Burns had no idea. Rio raised his brows. "What?"

Jerking his thumb over his shoulder, Burns said, "There aren't any drugs here."

Tori's presence here tonight had nearly floored him. This news was about to finish him off. He charged past Burns. "What are you talking about?"

Burns kicked one of the bags and several colorful *matryoshka* dolls tumbled onto the floor. Rio scooped up one of the dolls and pulled off the top. "These are nesting dolls. Did you check them all?"

Burns pointed to a pile of rounded pieces rocking on the floor. "That's what we've been doing. Apparently, it's a big surprise to Swain, too, although he won't admit it."

The murdered waiter last night. Tori's presence at the drop. Dolls instead of drugs. Alexi knew the CIA had him within range. Rio pounded his fist into his hand. They wouldn't nail him this time. What did that mean for Tori? For Max?

Who was he kidding? He knew exactly what it meant. His gaze wandered toward Tori, shoved into line with the others heading out of the house, hands shackled. She glanced over her shoulder, her eyes wide and glassy.

She knew exactly what it meant, too.

TORI DUCKED INTO THE van and inched her way along the bench in the back to make room for the others crowding inside. The side of her head throbbed where that idiot had smacked her with his gun.

Rio's fierce expression had both frightened her and given her hope. She'd had to stop him in his tracks before he blew everything, but the fact that he'd wanted to come to her rescue meant that he knew Alexi had coerced her participation in the so-called drug deal.

And that created a warm glow around her heart, despite the blow to her head.

When Alexi had come to her room after dinner, she'd been afraid he wanted to renew his passionate kisses. He'd had something worse in mind.

To prove her loyalty and willingness to work with him to return to Glazkova with Max, he'd invited her to go with his men on a business trip. He'd made it clear that if she refused, she wouldn't be winning the all-expenses-paid trip back to Glazkova.

Now what? Alexi had fooled them all. Discovering the possibility that a mole had infiltrated the catering staff, he had swapped the drugs he was going to sell to Grant for those little nesting dolls. What could the CIA prove from that? Only that Grant was stupid enough to pay hundreds of millions of dollars for some babushka dolls.

Now Alexi had free rein to leave Maui…and take Max with him. And he expected her to go along.

One of the agents stuck his head into the back of the van, now rank with sweat and fear—mostly hers. "Just because your drug deal didn't work out how you planned it, boys, doesn't mean we can't keep you in jail for the night to trace that money…and those guns."

He slammed the door shut, and Alexi's men mumbled among themselves in Russian. Tori could understand enough Russian to realize the men hadn't known about

Alexi's switch. They were all breathing sighs of relief now, though.

The van jostled over the rough road before hitting smooth pavement. In less than an hour, the vehicle jerked to a stop, and the doors creaked open. The agents hustled them out of the van, yelling orders. Frantically searching for Rio, Tori scanned the law enforcement personnel waiting to greet them.

The agent in charge shoved Tori toward a female officer. "She's all yours. Bring her to room two and then leave her there for one of our guys to question."

The woman pressed her hand against Tori's lower back, guiding her forward. "I'm Officer Garrett."

Tori kept her head down, her hair shielding her face. She'd been a fool to trust Alexi, but what options had he left her?

Officer Garrett pulled a key ring from her belt loop and unlocked a metal door and then unshackled Tori. "In here."

Stepping into the stark, chilly room, Tori clutched her upper arms. A solid table dominated the center of the room, three uncomfortable straight-back chairs crowding its edges. The airless space had no windows, but a large mirror took up almost one wall. Who lurked on the other side of that mirror?

"Have a seat. Someone will be right with you."

What, no strip search? "Thanks." Tori rubbed her arms and plopped onto a wooden chair.

A sharp rap sounded on the door and Officer Garrett opened it a crack before swinging it wide. She whispered a few words and then slipped out.

When Rio clicked the door behind him, Tori almost rushed into his arms. Instead she glanced at the two-way mirror and murmured, "Is it safe?"

"Safe enough." Rio pulled out the chair across from her, his back to the mirror, and placed a cup of tea in front of her. "The other agents know who you are now, and we didn't tell the local cops any more than they need to know."

Tori buried her face in her hands. "I'm so sorry, Rio."

"What for?" He shoved the tea toward her. "I'm guessing Alexi strong-armed you into going out with his guys."

She nodded, curling her fingers around the cup. "Max. It's always Max. He uses our son to control me. I'm sick of it."

"He found out we had him made." Rio ran a hand through his long hair. "Do you think he knows you had a hand in it?"

"I don't think so. He wants me to go back to Glazkova with him…and Max. To prove my loyalty to him and my commitment, he ordered me to go on this drop. Since he sent the dolls instead of the drugs, he knew I wouldn't get into any real trouble over this."

"True enough." Rio rubbed the stubble across his jaw, and then pinched the bridge of his nose. "I hate to be the one to tell you this, Tori, but he's going to use this opportunity to spirit Max back to Glazkova."

Fear leaped like a flame in her chest. "What opportunity?"

"Your incarceration."

"My incarceration?" She flattened her sweaty palms on the surface of the table, trying to steady her hands.

"We're holding these guys for a few days. The circumstances of the meeting permit it—the weapons, the cash. If we hold them, we have to hold you, or at least pretend to hold you. You can't return to Alexi's estate or he'd suspect your involvement."

The meaning of Rio's words hit her like a sledgehammer, and she dropped her head to the table. She'd feared this scenario, had warned Rio about it. If the CIA couldn't bring down Alexi fast and hard, he'd disappear and take Max with him.

Her head shot up, and she narrowed her eyes. "It's like I told you before, Rio. We have to rescue Max."

"How?" He tapped his long fingers on the table, close enough to her hand that she felt a whisper of his touch.

All too aware of the two-way mirror, she ignored the feelings that touch ignited. "I know the layout of the place, and I know Max's routine." She drew her hands into fists and straightened her spine. "I know when Ivan goes to bed, and I know who's there with him."

"Are you suggesting a kidnapping?"

She twisted her hair around her hand and threw it over her left shoulder. "I always knew it would come to this. Didn't you…cowboy?"

Tori held her breath waiting for his protests. She needed him, but she'd attempt the rescue with or without Rio McClintock.

He nodded slowly. "I suppose so. Protective custody will be the safest place for you while I carry out the rescue."

"Oh, no, you don't." She smacked her hands on the table. "You're not rescuing my son without me. There's no time. As soon as we have him, we need to leave. I'm not going to risk the CIA getting involved and using Max as a pawn to lure Alexi into some kind of trap."

By the way Rio's spiky, dark lashes fell over his eyes, Tori knew she'd hit the target. She scooted her chair closer to the table, allowing her knees to bump his. She hooked her foot around his ankle. "Please, Rio. I need to be in on the abduction. I won't slow you down. I know how to handle a weapon. I'm in good physical condition. And I'm motivated."

She could feel the pressure of Rio's knees against hers as he studied her from beneath lowered eyelids. "Can you row?"

Her leg jerked. "What?"

"A boat. Can you row a boat?"

"Hell, yes. I grew up in the great outdoors."

She had? He'd always figured her for a princess through and through. "We take a Zodiac in to keep it quiet. Stay close to the shoreline. I can get one of my buddies from the Agency to meet us around the bend with a power boat and another to pick us up via helicopter farther out once we have Max."

She blinked several times and licked her lips. "How do we get into the house?"

"We'll figure it all out once we get you out of here, but we have to move fast. Alexi will probably hightail it off Maui before the police release his guys and you from jail."

She shoved back from the table and hunched forward. "What are we waiting for?"

"We need to sneak you out of here so none of Alexi's men see you. With a few of his guys in the slammer, Max's rescue should be easier." The comforting words rolled off Rio's tongue. Nothing about this operation would be easy. Tori's tight mouth and narrowed green eyes showed she didn't buy a word of it.

Crossing her arms, she asked, "Where are you going to stash me until game time?"

Rio raised his brows. "You're coming home with me."

TORI GRIPPED HER UPPER arms as a creeping warmth spread to her cheeks. Why had this sudden modesty flashed through her body? She'd been waiting to hear those words from Rio's lips ever since he dragged her down that hill and she got a look at his deep brown eyes. Dropping her arms, she tilted up her chin. "Not the hotel. I'd be a little conspicuous there."

"No. My former digs before I upgraded. I gotta warn you though, where we're going you can't order a massage on demand…you might have to wait five minutes while I find my hot oil."

Tori grinned for the first time in hours. "What are we waiting for?"

Working with the local cops, Rio spirited Tori out of the station and into his rental car. Tori slumped in the passenger seat with a hat pulled low over her eyes while Rio checked his mirrors and wound his way through detours to make sure no headlights suddenly appeared behind them.

Tori slid a sideways glance his way. "That drug-bust-that-never-was made life a lot harder for you, didn't it?"

He shrugged as he adjusted his own hat. "Blew my cover, but then I don't intend on hanging around too much longer."

Rio swung his rental car off the main highway onto a smaller road where the headlights from the car illuminated lush vegetation. He turned onto a dirt road that climbed a sloping incline before parking the car in front of a small house set down beneath an old, twisted banyan tree.

Tori hoisted herself up and leaned forward. "This is beautiful. Why would you ever want to leave this place for that soulless resort in Kaanapali?"

"To look after you." Rio pushed the car door open and swung his keys around his finger. "Come on. We have a lot of planning to do."

Hours after midnight, as the moon touched the crest of the hillside with gold, Tori sat curled up in the corner of the sofa, her hands wrapped around a mug of tea. She'd just listened to Rio on the phone with his two CIA contacts discussing powerboats, Zodiacs and helicopters. They made it sound so easy, but she knew better.

The furrow between Rio's brows told her the truth.

"He'll kill you." She gazed into the brandy-colored tea, unable to meet Rio's eyes.

"He has to catch me first." Rio kicked his legs onto the coffee table, folding his arms behind his head, and yawned. "I've been doing this kind of work for a while, Tori. Trust me."

"I do trust you, Rio."

"Do you have enough faith in me to take my advice and stay out of this? You can go with Derrick on the helicopter. I'll bring Max to you."

"Max will never go with you." She clinked her cup on the table. "I have to be there or he'll put up a fuss. Who knows? He may even put up a fuss with me. I haven't had enough time with him to gain his trust."

"You're his mother. That's a bond that can withstand the toughest test."

"You sound like you speak from experience. Did your relationship with your mother withstand a lot?" Tori hadn't heard much about Rio's mother from the McClintocks—just that she'd left Silverhill when she found out about her pregnancy.

Closing his eyes, Rio leaned his head back. "My mother was flighty, irresponsible. I never knew my father, but he already had a family."

Rio's lips twisted in a bitter smile, and Tori wanted to reach out and smooth away his pain. She knew Rio could have that family for the asking. The McClintock brothers, Rio's half brothers, would accept him as one of their own in a heartbeat. Well, Rafe, the youngest, would anyway. Rod and Ryder would eventually come around.

Tori doubted the wisdom of keeping her knowledge of his family a secret. Would he feel betrayed? Maybe, but she couldn't spring that on him now. *Coward.*

She traced a pattern on the rough denim covering her thigh. "So she left your father?"

"Onto the next adventure." He sat forward and snapped his fingers. "Just like that. While she was pregnant she joined a commune in New Mexico where I was born, and then it was 'have baby knapsack, will travel.' She jaunted all over the country with me strapped to her body."

"She must've loved you a lot to keep you with her like that."

He shrugged. "I think the novelty of a baby wore off quickly. She'd leave me with friends, boyfriends and even relative strangers while she worked as a waitress, ski instructor, stripper and even a bit-part actress when we got to L.A. She pursued her dreams at the expense of mine."

Tori's fingers inched toward his hand, clenched into a fist. She traced over his knuckles. "And what were your dreams?"

"Stability, family, going to the same school for one solid year instead of being the new kid all the time."

"Life's funny, huh?" She closed her hand over his fist. "I had all that growing up and I threw it all away for a life of excitement and adventure. I guess it's a case of being careful what you wish for. So when you grew up, why didn't you seek the life you desired as a child? Why join the military and become a spy? Why not an engineer or a doctor?"

"Because it's all I knew." He placed his other hand on top of hers, sandwiching it between his own. "I turned out just like my mother—rootless, disconnected, on the move."

"Well, not exactly like her."

Rio tilted his head, his dark eyes like pools of melted chocolate.

"You were never a stripper, were you?"

He threw back his head, his loud laugh bouncing off the walls of the little house. Without releasing his hold, he dragged her into his lap. "You're amazing, Tori Scott. We're hours away from staging a dangerous rescue of your son, and you can still laugh."

"I learned a long time ago, if I couldn't laugh I'd drown in my tears." She wound her arms around his neck. "It's going to be okay, isn't it, Rio? We're going to get Max?"

His hands encircled her waist, his thumbs resting on her ribcage. "I promise we're going to get him out of there, but we're going to need some rest first. The sun's already coming up."

Snuggled in Rio's lap, her heart racing at his warm touch, Tori hadn't given a thought to rest. Just like in the hotel room, Rio was shutting her down. She slid from his lap, disappointment lancing her belly. "B-before I take a nap, I'd like to take a shower. This place does have a shower, doesn't it? I didn't notice one in the bathroom."

Rio grinned. "I'll take you to the shower."

Grabbing her hand, he shot up from the sofa and tugged her toward the back of the house. He threw open the backdoor and pointed to a showerhead rigged to a pipe and poised above a square of tiles.

Tori's jaw dropped. "You weren't kidding about the rustic nature of this place. Is that outdoor contraption really the only shower?"

"Change your mind? You don't have to worry about privacy. There's no reason for anyone to come down this road and after I get you a towel, I promise to wait inside. Then it's my turn."

Tori turned toward him and bunched his T-shirt in her fists. "Let's conserve water."

His hands caressed her shoulders, a questioning light in his dark eyes.

"I know you didn't want to mix business with pleasure when we were at the hotel, at least I hope that's the reason you left me hanging off a cliff." She yanked at his shirt. "But who knows what's going to happen tomorrow, Rio? I can't just let this…whatever this is between us… dry up and blow away. Can you?"

Rio's eyes grew as black as molten lava and then a smile split his face. He jerked away from her grasp and jumped off the wooden step of the porch. "Last one in has to go back for the towels."

Tori screamed and scrambled after him, following the trail of his discarded clothing. By the time she reached the shower, Rio had cranked on the water and steam wafted across his naked body as the hot water collided with the cooler air.

Her fingers trembled as she unbuttoned her jeans and peeled the rest of her clothes from her body. Rio sluiced back his long hair, and Tori's gaze followed the rivulets of water running across the flat planes and hard muscles of his body.

He extended his hand. "Come in. The water's fine."

She laced her fingers with his and, on tiptoes, joined him on the rough slab of cement. Rio pulled her flush against his wet body as the warm water from the showerhead cascaded down her back.

His heartbeat thundered through her frame, and she clung to him, resting her cheek on his chest. The warmth of his body melted away the tension of walking on eggshells with her own son and telling lipstick lies to her deadly ex-husband.

If the rescue tonight didn't work out the way they planned, at least she'd have this moment of solitude with Rio in the glory of the breaking dawn. If she had to go back to Glazkova with Alexi, she'd have the memory of Rio's touch to heat her blood in the dead of the chilly Glazkovian winter.

Rio wedged a finger beneath her chin, tilting back her head. "I promise."

He kissed her eyelid and the curve of her jaw. As he brushed his lips against hers, the sweet kiss sent ripples of desire along her spine. His hands followed, his rough palms sweeping down her back, resting on the curve of her hips. He hitched her closer and deepened his kiss.

His potent desire stabbed her belly, and she dug her fingernails into the hard muscles of his buttocks to keep from slithering down the drain with the water.

He reached over her shoulder to grab a small bottle of shampoo from the shower caddy, precariously swinging from the showerhead. He squeezed a puddle in his palm and said, "Turn around."

She peeled her body from his and shuddered as she presented her back to him. He worked the shampoo into her hair with strong fingers, massaging her scalp and showering kisses on the back of her neck.

She closed her eyes as he tilted her head under the

spray of water. "Mmm, I don't think the hotel offers this service."

"They'd better not." He squeezed her hair, tugging slightly. "How about that other place?"

"The other place?" She turned in his arms, grabbing the sliver of soap and lathering his chest.

"The compound." He clasped her wrists in midswirl. "Did that ex-husband of yours offer to...lather you up? Is that part of his package deal to Glazkova?"

She slid out of his grip. Did Rio really believe she'd make that deal with Alexi? "Alexi just wants to exert his control over me again. He's not interested in anything more intimate."

He took a step back, his gaze sweeping down her naked body like a featherlight brush on her skin. "Yeah, right. I find that hard to believe."

"Really?" Her soapy hands continued their path across his chiseled chest and outlined his six-pack. "And why is that?" she purred in a husky voice as her fingertips teased his tight, silky erection.

Squeezing his eyes shut, Rio drew a breath between clenched teeth. "Fishing for compliments, princess?"

She trailed her fingernails along the insides of his thighs. "Fishing for something."

She had no intention of allowing Rio McClintock to slip from her grasp this time.

He cinched her wrists and pulled her close for a soapy kiss. "I don't mind showering in the great outdoors, but I draw the line at...other activities."

Twisting the handle, he turned off the water and Tori shivered. "You're not really going to send me inside to get the towels, are you?"

He draped an arm across her shoulders and molded

the side of her body against his. "Who needs a towel when we have body heat?"

Her curves fitted snugly against his hard planes. Arms twined around each other, they strolled back to the house. Tori didn't even notice the cool morning air raising goose bumps on her flesh. Once inside the house, Rio snagged two towels from the cupboard and rubbed Tori's back with one of them. She returned the favor, making sure some parts of his body were drier than others.

With a grunt, he scooped her up in his arms and carried her into the claustrophobic bedroom. She didn't mind the size of the room because it felt like they were the only two people in the world—far from the compound, far from Glazkova, far from the tension that gnawed at her gut every time she thought of Max.

They fell across the double bed, which occupied most of the space in the room. Rio sealed his body to hers for warmth and she melted against him, soaking up his strength and fortitude. After thoroughly kissing her mouth, he ducked beneath the covers and brought the pleasure of his lips to other areas of her anatomy.

Her limbs trembled as another type of strength surged through her body. Giving in and letting go to this man, Tori had never felt more in control because she sensed his surrender to her, too.

When he entered her, their bodies moved in a natural rhythm. Everything that had happened in her life brought her to this moment with this man…and Tori didn't regret one minute of any of it.

Her climax rushed through her, and Rio's warm breath caressed her cheek. "Open your eyes."

Her lashes fluttered open and her passion intensified as she met Rio's dark gaze. A light flared in his eyes, and he drove into her, claiming her as his own.

They collapsed in a tangle of sheets, and Tori rolled onto her side, resting her head on Rio's shoulder. Her fingers skimmed along his mocha skin, unable to resist the lure of his perfect form.

He weaved his fingers through hers and kissed her knuckles. "We need to get some sleep to be sharp and well rested for tonight."

She yawned and nibbled on his salty earlobe. "As long as you sleep right by my side."

"I'm not going anywhere, princess."

"And after the rescue? Will you stay with me…with us then?" Tori bit her lip, afraid to meet his eyes.

The hand he'd been rubbing in circles on her lower back stilled. "You want me to stay with you?"

"J-just until we're safe. You do work as a bodyguard sometimes, don't you? I could pay you."

He drew in a sharp breath, his body stiffening. "You don't have to pay me. I'll see you safely wherever you want to go."

"I didn't mean to offend you, Rio. I just want you to know that this," she gestured at their tangled limbs, "is separate from Max's rescue. That's a job, your job. This is pure pleasure."

He let out a long breath and tugged at the back of her hair to turn her head toward him. The corner of his mouth lifted as he gazed at her through half-closed eyes. "This is pure pleasure."

She grinned and kissed the edge of his smile. "Then let me pay you for your services…I mean your bodyguarding services. It's more for my benefit than yours."

"The CIA is still paying me well for this job and you're part of the job." He plowed his fingers through her tangled, damp locks. "Once we rescue Max, where to?"

"I can go anywhere I want, right?"

"Anywhere the private jet can fly. Anywhere you think you and Max can hide out from your ex."

Tori swallowed and rested her chin on his chest. "I want to go home, back to where I grew up, back to where I feel safe."

"And where is home, Tori Scott? Where do you feel safe?"

Maybe she should give him the first answer that popped into her head at that question—right here in his arms. She squeezed her eyes shut and draped her arm around his body to soften the blow.

"Silverhill, Colorado."

Chapter Twelve

Rio blinked, the haze of sex and desire evaporating, leaving a chill on his sweat-moistened skin. Did Tori just say *Silverhill, Colorado*, his own private version of hell on earth?

"Huh?" He shifted beneath her, propping up his back against the wicker headboard. The point of her chin slid down to his belly, and her hair created a veil across her face.

"Silverhill, Colorado." She repeated the words, muffled against his stomach, but he heard them as if she'd shouted them in his ear.

"Are you telling me you grew up in Silverhill?" He grabbed fistfuls of sheet and held on.

"Yes." She rolled her head to the side, finally meeting his gaze, her eyes open and clear—maybe for the first time since he'd met her.

Tori's long hair trailed between his legs, tickling him, arousing him once again despite the chasm of foreboding widening in his gut. He swung his legs over the side of the bed and planted his feet firmly on the floor—maybe since the first time he'd met her.

"You know my...my half brothers." He'd uttered a statement, not a question. Of course she knew the almighty McClintocks of Silverhill. So the question remained, since she knew the indispensable McClintock brothers, why in the hell had she tracked *him* down?

And why had she seduced him?

"I do know your brothers. Rafe's wife, Dana, was one of my closest friends growing up." She yanked the covers up to her chin, leaving him in the cold.

He grabbed the edge of the bed, digging his fingers into the mattress. "Why'd you lie?"

"I didn't lie." She scrambled to sit next to him, pressing her thigh against his. "I just didn't think it would be wise to give you all the details—too much of a distraction."

"You figured your connections to Silverhill and my so-called family would jeopardize your chances of getting me to help you." He inched away from her warmth and the sweet hibiscus scent in her hair.

"Okay. I admit once I found out…"

Her words trailed off as he twisted his head to the side and skewered her with a sharp gaze through narrowed eyes. "You thought you'd find another McClintock on that hillside watching your ex-husband?"

Biting her lower lip, she nodded. "My conversation with Dana was breaking up. When she mentioned the CIA was in Maui tracking Alexi, I figured she meant Ryder. When I hiked out to the backcountry that day, I expected to find Ryder McClintock…your brother."

"Half brother." He pushed off the bed and grabbed one of the damp towels they'd used less than an hour ago to dry each other's bodies, hands and mouths exploring, caressing, bringing pleasure. He wrapped the towel around his waist firmly, tucking in the end at his hip.

"Why'd you stick around once you realized you had the wrong McClintock? Why didn't you go running back to your childhood friends for help?"

"You were here. They weren't." She lifted a smooth

shoulder, and the sheet slid down on one side, half exposing the curve of her breast. "What does it matter, Rio?"

He paced to the window, a muscle ticking in his tight jaw like a time bomb. He couldn't give voice to his fear—a fear born of childhood insecurities. His half brothers had known Tori first, had grown up with her. Hell, maybe even one of them had dated her, bedded her. They were there first and he was second best…like always.

"You should've gone back to your precious Silverhill." He smacked the wall with his fist, and the little room almost trembled with his fury. Those old feelings could wash over him so quickly, unwanted and unbidden. "You should've asked one of the real McClintocks to help you instead of settling for the next best thing."

Her wide green eyes softened, and she clambered out of the covers twisted around her body. "I didn't need their help. I needed your help. I need you."

She stood before him naked, her lush body his for the taking. Desire burned hot in his belly while arousal mixed with a fierce possessiveness pounded in his veins. He hooked an arm around her waist, cupping one perfectly rounded breast in his hand. The pad of his thumb skidded across her nipple, and then he froze in midcaress.

His hands flew to her shoulders and his fingers bit into the soft flesh. He shoved her to her knees and growled, "Get under the bed."

TORI'S KNEES BANGED AGAINST the hardwood floor, and her hands followed as Rio shoved her toward the bed. Was this some kind of weird punishment for lying to him?

"Someone's outside." His whisper sent a cascade of chills along her spine, and she scrambled across the floor and scooted under the bed, grabbing a damp towel on her way. Flattening her body against the floor, she tucked the towel around her and pulled the bedclothes across the gap.

Rio's bare feet padded into the other room, the distinctive sound of a safety being released from a gun resounding through the little house.

Tori swallowed, her dry mouth causing her to choke. If one of Alexi's men found her here, Alexi would know the police had released her...and the only reason the cops would do that is if she'd been part of the setup.

She held her breath as rustling noises came from the other room. Resting her forehead on the cold floor, she tensed her muscles. The front door creaked and Tori clenched her hands, digging half moons into her palms. *Please be careful, Rio.*

Several seconds ticked by, and then the bedroom window slid open. Adrenaline pumped through Tori's still form, and she panted with the effort to regulate her breathing. Was Rio at the window?

No, not Rio. Rio wouldn't climb through the window of his own house. As the intruder dropped to the floor with a thud, Tori clenched her teeth against the scream gathering in her lungs. Stealthy footsteps circled the bed. Tori squeezed her eyes shut. Maybe she should warn Rio. If this person creeping around the room had a weapon, Rio could stumble right into a trap.

Cool air brushed the bottoms of her feet, and she emitted an involuntary gasp. Then calloused fingers cinched her right ankle. Tori screamed as her attacker yanked her leg, dragging her from beneath the bed as her fingernails clawed at the smooth wood, desperate for purchase.

She twisted in the man's grasp, rolling onto her back and desperately clutching the towel around her body. Kicking out with her free leg, she smacked against a booted ankle. She tried to sit up, but the man jerked her leg higher and she fell back, her shoulder blades slamming against the floor.

Gasping in pain, she renewed her assault with her left foot, driving her heel against the man's kneecap. He grunted and aimed the butt of his gun at her head.

"Keep still, Princess Victoria, or I'll deliver you to your husband unconscious, as well as naked."

She raised her head, pushing the hair out of her face. Her jaw fell open as Ivan smirked. She fell back against the floor and spread the towel across her body to protect herself from Ivan's leering grin.

A shadow moved beyond the door.

"Let go." She jiggled her leg. "Alexi might kill you for your impure thoughts alone."

Fear darkened the man's eyes as he uncurled his blunt fingers from around her ankle. She whipped to her side, kicking at the weapon in Ivan's hand. He cursed and swung his arm back toward her, but the menacing figure behind him snatched his arm and bent it behind Ivan's back.

Tori heard a snap and Ivan screamed in agony, dropping to his knees. Rio loomed above him and cracked the butt of his gun on the back of Ivan's head. Ivan collapsed face-forward onto the floor, a trickle of blood oozing from his wound.

Tori jumped up and yanked a T-shirt from a hanger in Rio's open closet just as the towel around Rio's waist dropped to the floor. She slipped the T-shirt over her head, a grin forming on her trembling lips. "Do you think one of us might stay clothed?"

Rio snorted as he scooped up Ivan's gun lying use-lessly next to him. "Throw me some shorts. "I'd rather not be buck naked while cuffing another man. That'd be so wrong on so many levels."

A giddy giggle escaped her lips as she reached for a pair of Rio's shorts hanging over the single chair in the room.

Rio stepped into the shorts and then trained his gun on Ivan's inert form. "Tori, there's a pair of handcuffs in my black backpack by the front door."

She sailed into the other room, found the cuffs and handed them to Rio. "How did he find you here?"

Rio shrugged as he dragged Ivan's body toward the radiator and cuffed his wrist to it. "Nothing is foolproof, but I'm not firing on all cylinders. He used one of the oldest tricks in the book on me tonight. He hung some wooden wind chimes on a branch away from the house, and I followed the noise, leaving you unprotected."

Was he blaming her for distracting him or blaming himself for being distracted? Either way the grim set of his jaw signaled regret. She hugged herself in the baggy T-shirt, and Rio's scent, which clung to its folds, engulfed her. "What now?"

"I'm going to call my contacts at the Agency to pick him up and warn them not to put him back in the general jail population with the others. The men we arrested could still contact Alexi. As long as we keep Ivan iso-lated, he won't be giving away our little secret."

Tori blew out a breath and sank onto the edge of the bed. "At least we'll have one less security person to deal with, and Ivan was the one keeping an eye on Max."

"Let's have some breakfast and then get some rest after the CIA picks up this guy." He aimed a foot at Ivan's broad back.

"Rio, about Silverhill…"

"Save it." He sliced his hand through the air, cutting off her explanation.

Tori gnawed on her bottom lip. Would he still accompany her and Max to Colorado? Or would he allow his pride and insecurities to stand in the way of what they felt for each other?

She narrowed her eyes as she watched Rio on the phone to his CIA buddies. Because Rio McClintock could push her away as much as he wanted, but she knew how he felt about her.

Nobody had ever kissed and touched her the way Rio McClintock just had. And that meant something.

Rio brushed a lock of hair from Tori's face, the silken strands sliding through his fingers. He hated waking her for the task ahead. What if they failed to rescue her son? What if *he* failed?

And what if they succeeded? Could he really just put her on a plane to Colorado and walk out of her life? Of course, she'd have the mighty McClintocks to keep her safe.

"Tori." He rubbed her back. "Tori, it's time."

Her lashes fluttered, and a sigh escaped from her lips. Rio skimmed the pad of his thumb along her soft cheek, warm from the pillow. He wanted to kiss her plump lips, awaken her with his embrace and then claim her as his own all over again.

Instead he gritted his teeth and shook her. His uncontrollable desire for this woman had landed them both in trouble. His thinking these past few days had been emanating from another part of his anatomy and not his brain.

When the big Glazkovian, Ivan, had come to, he'd

admitted that he'd been lurking outside the police station after the CIA had brought in Swain's and Alexi's men. He'd recognized Rio as the man from the park and clipped a tracking device on his car.

Rio's feelings for Tori had put her in danger. He shook Tori harder. "Wake up."

She rolled onto her back and peeled open one eyelid. "What time is it?"

"It's time to rescue Max. Everything's in place." Or at least everything would be in place once he got his professionalism back on track.

She reached out for him and slid her hand along his thigh. "I'm scared, Rio."

"Then don't go." He pushed off from the bed and grabbed his backpack. "You can wait on the boat or go up in the helicopter. I'll bring Max to you."

Her brows collided over her nose, and she dug her fists into her eyes. "I have to be there for Max."

Rio snatched the small but deadly Beretta from his bag and extended it, handle first, to Tori. "You said you knew how to use a gun, right? After all, you're from Silverhill, Colorado."

Sitting up, she tilted her head, her brow furrowed. "I do know how to use a gun. I've also been practicing martial arts. I've been preparing for this moment for the past two years of my life."

His gaze dropped from her puzzled green eyes to the soft curve of her breasts beneath his T-shirt. He had a hard time envisioning Tori as a lean, mean fighting machine. He swallowed. "Good. Your clothes from last night will work perfectly for our mission. I…uh…collected them from the lawn and they're dry. You should wear the stocking cap, too."

She swung her legs over the side of the bed, tugging

the T-shirt over her thighs. Her gaze darted to the black jeans and T-shirt folded on the chair, her underwear stacked neatly on top. "Great. I'll get dressed and…"

He pointed to the bathroom. "There may not be an indoor shower in this place, but there's a sink. You can wash up and brush your teeth in there."

He practically lurched for the bedroom door, and then snapped it behind him on Tori's flushed face. He shouldn't have reminded her about the outdoor shower. He cursed his visceral response to her body. He shouldn't have reminded himself.

While Rio sliced some fresh fruit, he kept one ear trained on the bedroom. From the banging noises in there, it sounded like Tori was dismantling the place. She shoved open the door, and it almost flew off its hinges.

"Let's blow this shack." Her arms folded across her chest, she wedged a shoulder against the doorjamb.

"We need to eat something before we go." He waved his knife at the fragrant mangos, pineapple and papaya fanned out on the platter like a rainbow.

With a scowl marring her pretty features, Tori stabbed a hunk of pineapple with a fork and popped it into her mouth. The juice moistened her lips, and Rio wanted nothing more than to kiss its sweetness from her mouth.

He turned with an inward groan, digging deep for that professionalism he'd just promised himself. He gripped the handle of the coffeepot and poured himself a cup, the robust smell of the fresh brew like a slap in the face. "Coffee?"

"Sure." She ripped open a granola bar and broke off a piece. "Can we review the game plan once more?"

"We meet Ted at the marina and he'll take us by boat to the bay around the tip from Alexi's place. We take the Zodiac into the water and motor around the point. Then row to the shore beneath the compound. And then here's where it gets tricky." He slurped a sip of coffee letting it pool on his tongue before swallowing it. "We climb up the side of that cliff and haul ourselves onto the property."

"And if anyone's patrolling the lawn, we shoot him with the dart guns."

"Right. Save the real bullets for when your life is in danger."

"Or for when *your* life is in danger." She arched a brow at him before spearing a slice of papaya.

"Yeah, that, too." He'd feel a lot better if Tori manned the boat and Ted came with him on the mission, but she refused to be left behind. "Then we climb up to the balcony of that playroom, break in and slip into Max's room."

"Are you sure you can get Max down that cliff on your back?" She dropped the fork and crumbled the granola bar between her fingers.

"I've rescued full-grown men this way before. I can handle a four-year-old boy."

Tori's gaze wandered across the breadth of his shoulders and skimmed down the length of his arms as if assessing his strength to carry out the deed. Seemed as if she'd switched gears into work mode, but her gaze still felt like a caress to him.

Shaking his head, Rio took another gulp of coffee, which scalded his throat, punishing him for the way his body reacted to her every glance.

He cleared his throat and said more gruffly than he intended, "Ted's waiting."

BY THE TIME THEY REACHED the marina, Tori's disgust with all men had her finger itching to pull the trigger on her dart gun and take out the whole lot of them.

How dare Rio make love to her like he did last night and then treat her like a fellow agent tonight? She sucked in her breath. Idiot.

That's what you are.

Rio's kisses mucked up her mind, scrambled her senses—not the prime condition for a daring rescue. At least he had his focus in the right place

They pulled up to the slip where a powerful boat bobbed in the water. The man on deck waved and hopped onto the boat ramp.

Rio formally introduced her to Ted, who had been present at the raid the night before. He looked her up and down with raised brows. "Are you sure you don't want to trade places? I'll anchor the boat. All you have to do is float."

Tori dug her hands into her hips. "Max is my son. He'd be terrified if two strangers attempted to abduct him in the middle of the night. His screams would bring a cadre of security down on your heads in a matter of seconds."

"We could always sedate him."

Tori shot a look at Ted filled with venom, and he backed up, glancing at Rio. "Just a thought."

"It's a dumb thought." She brushed past him and jumped onto the deck of the boat. The men murmured behind her and then joined her on deck.

Ted yanked the throttle on the boat, and the big motor churned the water in the slip. Rio pulled a black stocking cap out of his pocket and thrust it into her hands. "Put this on."

Tori pulled the cap over her head and stuffed her hair inside while Rio rummaged through his pack. He held up a small silver disc and unscrewed the lid.

"Let me smear some of this on your face. More than anything, a white face shines in the dark."

Tori closed her eyes, and the rough pads of Rio's fingers, smudged with a greasy substance, swept across her nose and cheeks. He crossed a T on her face, rubbing the black grease into her chin and forehead. He touched his finger to her nose. "You'll be fine."

She patted the weapon in her pocket. "I know."

When they got to the bay around the corner from the one beneath Alexi's estate, Ted cut the engine of the boat. Clouds obscured the moon, and the white caps peaked across the dark ocean. They hauled the Zodiac over the side of the powerboat and Rio and Ted exchanged last minute assurances and instructions.

Tori clambered off the boat and dropped into the Zodiac on silent feet. Rio followed, and the inflatable dipped under his weight. He gunned the outboard motor and maneuvered around the rocky point. Once on the other side, he cut the engine, and Tori picked up her oar to paddle toward the rocky coast. No boats patrolled the coast, and Alexi's lookouts would have a hard time spotting the Zodiac on this moonless night.

They hit the shore and dragged the boat onto the sliver of beach littered with pebbles from the cliffs that shot up at a sheer angle. Licking her lips, Tori rubbed her palms on her jeans.

"You ready?" Rio tossed her a pair of gloves.

She nodded and yanked on the gloves, wiggling her fingers into the ends. She grabbed Rio's arm as he slung his pack onto his back. "I-if anything happens to me tonight, don't stop. Get Max out and take him to Silverhill. My brother's there and the McClintocks will keep Max safe."

Rio compressed his lips, his jaw tightening. "Nothing's

going to happen to you or Max tonight. I'll make sure of it. You go first."

She stowed her weapons in her small pack and inserted the toe of her rock shoe into the first foothold. Did Rio think he was in some kind of competition with his brothers? She wasn't above using that knowledge to get him to be her bodyguard and see her safely to Silverhill. Sure, she wanted his protection, but she wanted a whole lot more from him. He just didn't seem willing to deliver.

Her foot slipped and she gasped, dangling from the scrubby bush she clutched in her hands.

Gloved fingers wrapped around her ankle and placed her boot on a secure ledge. "You're almost there. When you get to the top, grab on to the branches of the bushes where they're overhanging and pull."

A trickle of sweat skidded down her back as she eyed the jagged precipice above her. Her shoulders and calves burned, but she pushed herself forward. A clump of bushes loomed almost over her head and she reached up and planted her hands in their interior branches. A few sharp twigs stabbed her through her long-sleeved black T-shirt, but she ignored the pain and hoisted herself up.

"Do you have a grip on the branches?"

"Yes," Tori hissed through clenched teeth.

She felt Rio's hand wedge against her bottom, shoving her up toward the ledge. With her lungs bursting, she dug her knee into the dirt at the top and flung herself into the bushes.

She immediately spun around, reaching for Rio. He grabbed on to the same bush, and Tori bunched her hands into his T-shirt to yank him over.

They panted beside each other for several seconds,

and then Rio coiled his body into a crouching position. "Get your dart gun ready. We're going to run across the lawn toward the patio. Stay close behind me to condense our movement."

Tori pulled the dart gun from her bag and gripped it in her hand. She squatted in a ready position, like she was in the blocks for a fifty-yard dash. Her leg pressed against Rio's taut thigh muscles. The man reverberated power and purpose. She just hoped a little reverberated her way so her knees wouldn't crumple when she started to run.

Rio eased up and pinched her chin between his thumb and forefinger. "Don't stop for any reason. We're leaving here with your son."

Closing her eyes, Tori pressed her palm against her galloping heart. "I'm ready."

Rio lunged forward out of the bushes, and adrenaline zinged through Tori's veins as she followed in his wake. The wet grass squished beneath the soft rubber soles of her rock boots and the sound rang in her ears like a fire alarm. Ten more yards to the darkened patio before they started the next perilous phase up to the balcony.

Panting more from fear than exertion, Tori clamped her teeth to bite down on the sound of her gasping. The form in front of her stopped. Rio had reached the patio.

Tori kept her gaze pinned to his dark shadow as she sprinted the last few steps. Then a voice growled to her left, "Take one more step and I'll blow your head off."

Chapter Thirteen

A sob ripped from Tori's throat, but before she could even swing her dart gun in the direction of the voice, she heard the smack of a hand against skin, a grunt and a thud. She tripped, and her knee hit the edge of the tiled patio.

Rio hitched his hands beneath her arms, lifting her back onto her feet. He whispered, "Help me drag him to the bushes."

She spun around, her gaze picking out a body crumpled in a heap. Rio grabbed the man's arms, and Tori picked up his feet. They stuffed him under the thick foliage that ringed the patio. Rio reached over and yanked the dart from the side of the man's neck.

She opened her mouth, but Rio put a finger to his lips. He dug into his pack and pulled out a rope attached to a heavy rubber anchor. Looking both ways, he stepped back into the yard and swung the rope over his head. He found his target with a soft thud and yanked on the now-taut rope.

He may have objected when she called him *cowboy,* but he had just about the best lassoing form Tori had ever seen.

He motioned her toward the rope, and she crept forward, flexing her fingers still encased in the thin rock-climbing gloves. She grabbed the rope with both hands and tugged. Rio hoisted her from below, and she shimmied up the rope, hand over hand.

She hoisted herself over the balcony's edge and dropped to the tile below, her knee throbbing with each movement. She crouched in the corner, waiting for Rio, her eyes glued to the sliding glass door to the playroom. *So close.*

Rio materialized next to her, and his stealthy appearance startled her. The man moved like a jungle cat.

He swiftly coiled the rope and withdrew the next handy spy tool from his backpack. That pack resembled a magician's bag of tricks...Tori was waiting for the rabbit.

The glass-cutting tool in Rio's hand glinted in the darkness and Tori gasped. She sprang forward and grabbed Rio's forearm. "What if this door is wired for an alarm?"

"It's not." He scraped out a square with the blade. "I checked it out during the party."

Rio reached through the hole he punched out in the glass and flicked the lock. Then he etched out a similar one at the bottom of the door and released another lock.

Tori held her breath as the door whispered open. She jerked her thumb toward the connecting door to Max's bedroom. Rio slid through the door first, his weapon ready.

With her mouth dry, Tori edged into Max's room half expecting him to be gone from his bed. Warm relief washed through her body when she saw his tousled hair on the pillow. After the rigid tenseness of her muscles the past hour, she felt as if she'd melt, so she grabbed the doorjamb for support.

Rio shot her a quick glance beneath furrowed brows. "What's wrong?"

She shook her head and inched into the room. Her gaze darted toward the closed bedroom door as she tip-toed toward Max's bed. Even though the CIA had Ivan safely locked up, Tori knew another willing minion stood sentry in the hallway. One peep from Max and the guard would be through the door like a shot.

Tori crouched by the bed and squeezed Max's shoulder. "Sweetie, Mommy's here."

Max snuffled and rolled to his side.

Tori swept the hair from his eyes and kissed his sleep-warmed cheek. "Max. Wake up."

He stirred and blinked his eyes, which widened in horror. Tori's stomach flip-flopped. If she had to clap her hand over Max's mouth to keep him quiet, a little piece of her heart would dry up and blow away.

As Max's mouth yawned open, Rio rustled behind her and snatched off her cap. Her hair tumbled around her shoulders, and Max's gaping mouth snapped shut. With his eyes still taking up half his face, Max whispered, "Mommy?"

"Shh." She put her finger to her lips and smiled. "We're playing a game. You're going to come out and play with me tonight."

Max scrambled to a sitting position and pointed a finger at Rio. "Who's he?"

"He's my friend. He's going to play, too. Are you ready?" She frowned when she saw Max's lightweight pajamas. "We have to get him some warmer clothes."

"No time. I have a jacket for him and there are blankets on the boat."

Tori scooped up Max in her arms and froze. Two voices murmured outside the door. Rio gave her a shove toward the playroom and gestured toward Max's bed. He then took the pillows and stuffed them beneath the covers. From the door, it would look like the sleeping form of a child.

Clutching Max to her chest, Tori rushed into the playroom. Rio joined her at the sliding door. He hooked the anchor along the edge of the balcony and threw the rope over the side. "Can he slide down?"

"If you're at the bottom to catch him."

"I want you out of here first."

She clutched Rio's arm. Even if she didn't escape, she wanted Max out. "You need to be at the bottom in case he falls."

He sucked in the side of his cheek. "You'd better be right behind us."

Rio disappeared over the side of the balcony, and Max shrieked, "Where'd he go?"

"Shush. This is a quiet game. He climbed down a rope. Do you want to try? It's just like the pirate ship at the park."

Max nodded, his eyes shining. Thank God she had an adventurous boy.

Tori peered over the side at Rio waiting below, his arms outstretched. She lifted Max over the side and folded her hands over his on the rope. "Hang on and shimmy down. My friend will be at the bottom and he'll catch you if you fall."

Max snorted. "I'm not going to fall."

Tori scooted him down the rope and, with her heart racing, watched the top of his head as he descended. Rio caught him off the dangling end and gave Tori a thumbs-up sign.

She hoisted herself over the side and slid down without gaining a firm grip. As her right hand flew off the rope, she tightened her grasp with her left, hanging to the side like a trapeze artist. Max yelped below her.

She found the rope with her right hand again and continued her descent. Rio's hands curled around her waist when she hit the bottom. "I thought I was going to have to catch *you* there for a minute."

She giggled. Her body was so wound up, if they didn't get off of this compound soon she could probably twirl off on her own without the helicopter.

Rio dug into his magic pack once again and pulled out the harness. Tori dreaded this the most. She helped Rio secure the harness around his shoulders and buckled the straps in the back.

He knelt down next to Max. "Hi, Max. I'm Rio. I'm going to carry you across the lawn and then you're going to climb onto my back. Does that sound like fun?"

Max's lower lip jutted forward. "I'm not a baby. I don't need to be carried."

Rio patted him on the back. "I know that, dude, but it's part of the game."

Max narrowed his eyes, but Rio didn't give him any time to think about it. He hoisted him in his arms, crushing him against his body. Then he hunched forward and took off toward the cliff.

Tori followed closely, her gun clutched in her hand. If anyone tried to take Max from Rio now, she'd have no problem shooting to kill.

They reached the cliff, and Rio set Max on the ground. "Now here's the really cool part. You're going to be strapped on to my back as we climb down this cliff. I know you're a big boy and you can handle that."

Max licked his lips, his gaze darting over the edge of the cliff and back to Rio.

The rope they'd tagged up the side of the hill would

make climbing down a lot easier than the journey up, but Tori's heart galloped in her chest anyway. She lifted Max and fed his legs through the straps in the harness. When she snapped the last buckle, floodlights from the house began sweeping the lawn.

Fear spiraled down her spine. "Rio, the lights."

"I guess we wore out our welcome. Get moving, princess."

She grabbed the rope and shimmied over the side on her belly. Rio immediately followed, Max strapped to his back. Over the roar of the ocean below her, Tori heard shouts. Had they discovered Max was missing already? She'd been hoping for a head start.

Tori rappelled smoothly down the side of the cliff as she kept her eye on Max. Although the harness held him securely, he had his arms wound around Rio's neck.

Tori sobbed with relief as her feet hit the rocks of the beach. The Zodiac waited like a refuge. Rio landed beside her, and, with shaking hands, Tori unhitched the harness.

A grin spread across Max's pale face. "That was fun. Can we do it again?"

"Maybe another time." Rio gave Max a high five. "Now it's time for the boat, and I know you can handle that."

Max clambered into the Zodiac and Rio whipped a jacket out of his backpack. "Put this on."

Tori helped Max into the big windbreaker and fastened a life vest around him. Then she and Rio shoved the Zodiac into the water. A small wave bumped the side and sprayed Tori's face. She licked the salt water from her lips and grabbed an oar.

They rowed into the bay toward the point. Tori panted as she struggled against the choppy water. Then she gulped as she noticed lights bouncing along the edge of the cliff where they'd gone over.

She nudged Rio's arm where his muscles bunched with the effort of paddling and pointed. "They found our exit."

He shrugged and wiped the sweat from his brow. "They can follow, but they have no boat waiting for them and half of them don't look capable of rappelling down the side of a craggy cliff. You did great, by the way. I'm impressed."

Despite herself, Tori felt a warm glow suffuse her face. "When you grow up in the Rocky Mountains, a few volcanic cliffs aren't going to faze..."

She cut off her words, wishing she'd bitten her tongue. Every time she mentioned Silverhill, Rio's face grew tight. She studied his features, but he just smiled.

"Your son must've inherited that from you because he didn't make a peep on the way down."

Tori jumped as the sound of a gunshot echoed across the bay. She hissed, "They're shooting at us."

Rio glanced at Max shivering in the corner of the boat. "I think they're just shooting. I doubt they can see the Zodiac. Hey, dude, why don't you scrunch down in the corner a little more? You'll be warmer."

Max wiggled into the corner, and Tori reached over and folded the collar of the jacket to secure it around Max's neck. "You're doing great, Max."

As the Zodiac reached the point of the jetty that divided the two bays, Rio flicked on his flashlight twice in quick succession. He waited several seconds and repeated the code. The engine of the powerboat roared to life and the headlight beamed across the water.

"Ted is closer than I expected." Rio gunned the motor

of the Zodiac and maneuvered toward the powerboat bearing down on them.

A flutter of fear wafted through Tori's chest. What if Ted wasn't on the powerboat? What if Alexi's men had already discovered him?

The powerboat slowed as it edged near the Zodiac, the engine a low rumble. As the boat turned, its wake lifted the Zodiac, and Rio cut the engine.

Ted rushed to the side, and Tori felt dizzy with relief. Then she saw his face.

"They're on their way. Did you get caught up there?"

Rio hauled a protesting Max over his shoulder and fed him up to Ted. "Yeah, they either discovered Max was gone or they found the guy in the bushes. They must've radioed ahead to the boat."

He swept up Tori in his arms and swung her over the side of the powerboat. "You and Max stay down. We've got ourselves a boat race."

Max whined. "Mommy."

"It's okay, sweetie. It's just a game." She dragged a blanket from a locker at the end of the boat and wrapped Max in its musty folds. She hunched in the corner, her body shielding Max from the cool ocean breeze…and anything else that came their way.

Ted revved the engine of the boat and shot out into the open ocean. A few minutes later the whine of another engine echoed across the water.

A sharp crack pierced through the roar of the dueling engines. Rio stretched out on the deck and cocked his weapon over the side. He fired back as Ted put the boat into overdrive.

Tori squeezed Max with one arm as she pulled her weapon out with her other hand. They'd have to get through her to take Max.

The thwacking sound of a helicopter passed above, but Ted waved him off. He yelled to Rio, "I don't want the chopper to get hit. We'll need to deal with these guys before Derrick can position the bird."

Rio scrambled to the other side of the boat. "Light 'em up."

Ted swung the big search light on the boat toward the oncoming sound of the engine. The strong beam picked out Alexi's powerboat slicing through the water. Rio discarded his handgun for a semiautomatic rifle. He jumped up on the deck and sprayed the side of the other boat while a hail of bullets shot back at them.

Tori screamed, "Rio, get down!"

A small explosion boomed in the water, and curses and screams filled the air. Rio collapsed to the deck. "I hit their gas tank. Fire it up, Ted, and signal Derrick."

The boat lurched forward, and they left the acrid smell of smoke behind. By the time Alexi got another boat after them, they'd be in the helicopter. Tori slumped, her breath harsh in her throat.

She smoothed Max's hair back from his clammy forehead as he whimpered. She cooed, "It's okay. We're going for a ride in a helicopter next."

She shifted her gaze to Rio, still lying on the deck. He must have been exhausted. "Are you okay, Rio?"

He didn't respond. Tori's breath hitched in her throat as she shifted Max from her lap. "Rio?"

Scrambling to her hands and knees, Tori crawled to Rio's still form. His spiky, dark lashes lay on his cheeks, his breath ragged and short. "Oh, my God, Ted. I think Rio's been hit."

"Hang on." Ted aimed the spotlight into the night sky to signal the chopper and then cut the engine and began to fumble with the anchor.

Tori pushed Rio onto his back, revealing a dark stain spreading out from his left shoulder. Gulping, she ripped the neck of his T-shirt, her hands slick with Rio's blood. "He has a bullet wound in his shoulder."

Ted called back as he hauled the anchor overboard, and the helicopter's lights pierced through the sky. "Put pressure on the wound to stop the bleeding. I'll see what I can do when we get in the chopper."

Tori ripped the remainder of Rio's T-shirt from his body, bunched it up and pressed it against the oozing wound. She put her face close to his. "Open your eyes. Open your eyes, damn it."

The chopper suspended above them, a ladder unfurling toward the boat's deck. A man's dark face appeared over the side. "Bring the boy up first."

Her hands clamped over Rio's shoulder, Tori called out, "Ted."

He lifted Max. "Don't worry, Tori. I've got Max."

Ted clamped Max securely against his side as he climbed up the ladder to the chopper. Waiting hands pulled Max inside the helicopter. Ted jumped back onto the deck. "Go on up, Tori."

Tears flooded her eyes. Rio had put himself in the line of fire for her and Max. He'd shot out the gas tank of the other boat at the risk of his own life.

"I—I can't leave him, Ted."

He laid a hand on her back. "Rio's suffered worse than this little scrape. You did a good job staunching the wound. I'll take it from here. We all need to get in the helicopter...now."

Reluctantly, Tori peeled open her stiff fingers, stained with Rio's blood. Ted clamped his hand over the T-shirt and smacked Rio's face. "Wake up. Stop faking."

Rio's lids flickered, and he clenched his jaw. "Tori?"

"She's fine, and so's the boy. Now Derrick's getting mighty impatient up there in his bird, so haul your ass up and let's end this vacation."

Tori stumbled toward the ladder swaying in the wind and grabbed one rung. Ted slid an arm beneath Rio's good shoulder and heaved him to his feet. Rio staggered and almost fell backward. Then he shook his head and straightened his back. Clutching his shoulder, he shuffled toward the ladder.

Letting out a ragged breath, Tori clawed her way up and into the helicopter while steady hands grabbed her arms. She scooted back to the edge on her stomach and reached her arms out toward Rio climbing up the ladder with one hand, his left arm hanging uselessly at his side as Ted pushed him from beneath.

When Rio's head was level with the chopper, Tori reached down and hooked her arm beneath his right shoulder. She braced her feet against a bin in the helicopter and hauled him over the side as Ted wrapped his arms around Rio's legs and hoisted him up.

Rio grunted as he fell into the chopper. The man named Derrick flipped open a first aid kit and doused the wound with alcohol. Rio's breath hissed between his teeth.

Tori hovered over him, her fingertips smoothing a line down his jaw. "Is he going to be okay?"

Derrick nodded and grinned. "Once I get through with him. Now go sit down next to your son."

She knew a dismissal when she heard one. She secured Max in his seat and belted herself in the one next to him. She eyed Derrick as he pulled scary tools from his black bag and probed Rio's wound as he lay stretched out on the floor.

Ted lurched into the chopper and pulled up the ladder.

He smacked the side of the bird and shouted to Derrick's copilot, "Let's go."

The helicopter tilted and swept forward, back toward land, and Tori laced her fingers through Max's. Were they really safe? She wouldn't believe it until they hit the mainland and Rio was fully conscious and healed.

She looked out the window at the powerboat still bobbing on the water. "You're just going to leave the boat out there?"

"Not exactly." Ted pulled a switch from his pocket and waved it back and forth.

Tilting her head, Tori asked, "What's that?"

"Insurance."

He flipped the switch, and the boat exploded in the water, orange flames leaping from the oil slick on the surface of the ocean.

Tori swallowed. These guys didn't fool around.

Rio groaned as Derrick injected a needle into his shoulder.

"What are you doing? I thought you were a pilot, not a doctor."

Derrick looked up as he pulled out the needle. "I'm a man of multiple talents, and I have to remove the bullet. He doesn't have time for a stay in the hospital."

Doctor Derrick totally lacked a bedside manner. "Can I help?"

"Are you squeamish?"

"No." She unbuckled her seatbelt and patted Max's arm, tucking the blanket around him. "You doing okay?"

Max nodded sleepily, lulled by the buzz of the helicopter.

Tori crouched next to Rio and doused her hands with disinfectant. "Tell me what to do."

Rio faded in and out of consciousness as Derrick removed the bullet from his shoulder and cleaned and bandaged the wound. He pulled out a bottle of water and a couple of tablets. "Lift his head. He needs some antibiotics and painkillers."

Tori ran her hands through Rio's dark, tangled hair and propped his head on her knees as she massaged his temples with her thumbs. "Drink some water and take the pills. You're going to be all right."

Derrick placed the pills on Rio's tongue and held the bottle of water to his lips. He gulped down the water, and his lips quirked into a smile. "Thanks, Doc."

A tear slid down Tori's cheek, and she leaned over and kissed Rio's wet lips. He sighed with contentment and burrowed his head into her lap.

Derrick exchanged a look with Ted, which Tori ignored. She'd probably just ruined Rio's reputation as a tough guy.

Derrick shook out a blanket and covered Rio. "He should be falling asleep soon, which is the best remedy for him right now. We're taking this bird to a small airstrip in Honolulu, and Rio has a private Gulfstream ready. Where to?"

Tori caressed Rio's hair between her fingertips and tucked it behind his ear as she murmured, "Huh?"

"Where are you and your son going after this?"

Tori traced a finger along Rio's hard jaw, now slack with drowsiness. He might even sleep right through the plane ride. She jerked up her head, eyes wide. "Didn't Rio tell you? We're going to Colorado. Silverhill, Colorado."

Chapter Fourteen

The throbbing pain in his shoulder crept up his neck and pounded against his temples. Rio peeled his tongue from the roof of his mouth and ran it across his dry lips. Pinching the bridge of his nose, he squeezed his eyes shut as the pain zinged through his head.

He shifted, and the soft, cool pillow beneath him soothed his pulsating headache. His body vibrated slightly with the low hum of an engine. He rubbed his eyes. Derrick had dug that bullet out of his shoulder on the floor of the chopper. This ride was too smooth for a chopper over the ocean.

"He's awake." A woman's voice, low and musical, eased his aching soreness even more, and he floated on a pleasant dream before a twinge shot through his shoulder again.

He swallowed, but his parched throat caused him to choke. Cool hands fluttered about his face and shoulder. Capable fingers curled around the back of his neck, tilting his head up. "Can you drink something now, Rio?"

Another woman's voice, but not the one that had calmed his senses before. He struggled to sit up, and the cushions beneath his back rose to an incline. Someone pressed the rim of a glass to his lips, which he parted to accept the water tipped into this mouth.

He sipped slowly and then eased open his eyes, blinking against the low light of the aircraft's interior. A woman, her dark hair pulled back, swam into focus.

She smiled. "Welcome back, Rio. Derrick did a great job. You show no signs of fever and your bullet wound, while red, is not inflamed at all."

He curled his hand around the glass and took it from her. He took another swallow of water and cleared his throat. "Where's Derrick? Are Tori and Max okay?"

She pulled the blanket farther off his bare shoulder. "May I?" She didn't wait for his answer, pressing her hand against his gauze dressing. "Good, no moisture. Derrick's flying this plane, Max is sleeping two rows up and Tori's right behind me."

She shifted to her right, and Tori's head popped over her shoulder. "How are you feeling, Rio? This is Cora. She's a nurse, and Derrick called her in to accompany you back to the mainland."

Rio fell back, cradling the glass of water in both hands. "So you're safe? We got away from Maui okay?"

Cora moved into the aisle to grab a black leather bag from the seat across from his, and Tori took her place, crouching beside his reclining seat. She readjusted the blanket, yanking it up to his chin. "We're safe, thanks to you. If you hadn't literally blown their boat out of the water, I'm not sure how we would've gotten away."

He lifted his injured shoulder and winced. "Had to do it before they did it to us."

"Shortly after their tank exploded, Derrick brought the helicopter in and we all got inside, including Ted. He then blew up the boat. Derrick flew us over to Honolulu, called in Cora and we put you on the plane. We just took off over the Pacific. Ted stayed behind."

Cora returned with her palm open. She shoved three tablets beneath his tongue. "More antibiotics to keep an infection at bay. Swallow."

Rio sipped more water, and the tablets slid down his throat. Damn. He hated being out of control, loaded on the plane like an invalid, drugged up. "Is Max all right?"

"He's sleeping. He was confused and scared, but he'll be fine just as soon as I get him home." Tori turned her head, and her hair fell across her face.

Rio's brain, which had been clearing, seemed to fog over again. He struggled against the languor seeping through his body once again. The glass in his hand jerked, spilling drops of water onto the blanket.

Cora caught the glass from his hand as his grip relaxed. "Just go with the flow, Rio. I slipped you another sedative with the antibiotic. Your body needs sleep to heal."

Home. Home. Home. Tori's words floated through his brain, and he tried to latch on to them, tried to make sense of them. He concentrated every ounce of effort he had on forming his own words in his uncooperative mouth. Finally, he breathed out, "Where we going?"

Cora's voice pierced through the haze cloaking him. "We're going to Silverhill, Colorado."

RIO STARED OUT THE WINDOW as Cora patted his fresh bandage. "Looks better already. Are you still groggy? You have time to catch a little more sleep before we land."

"I'm wide awake now. Do *not* give me any more happy pills." He shot Cora one of his deadliest snarls, one that reduced bad guys to quivering blobs of jelly. She smiled her know-it-all nurse's smile.

After Cora packed her bag and moved across the aisle, Tori slid into the seat next to him. "You agreed to be our bodyguard, didn't you? For a price."

Yeah, and what a price.

Her guileless green eyes didn't show a hint of guilt, not one speck of consciousness regarding the rest of the conversation that had taken place after he'd agreed to protect her and Max. The part where she had dropped the bombshell that she called Silverhill home.

He had agreed to take the job, but hadn't he changed his mind after she'd given him the bad news? He chewed his bottom lip, drawing blood. No, he hadn't. They'd been interrupted by Ivan the Terrible before he could nix the agreement.

But she must've known he'd back out once she changed the rules of the game. Instead she'd taken advantage of his helplessness, packed him on the Gulfstream and headed for home. Her home.

Tori dipped a napkin in water and dabbed his lip. "Be careful. You're still dehydrated. Drink some more fluids."

He growled and snatched the napkin from her hand. "I'm dehydrated because you and Nurse Ratched over there drugged me."

Cora smirked, never raising her eyes from her magazine. "You needed rest, Rio. You lost some blood and your body was going into shock."

"My body's still in shock."

Tori grabbed his hand. "We still need you, Rio—Max and I. You rescued him. You risked your life to save us. I can't think of a better audition for a bodyguard."

Her thumb ran across his knuckles, and he closed

his eyes, savoring her closeness. She'd saved him, too. If she hadn't reacted so quickly after he'd been shot, he would've lost a lot more blood.

He brought her hand to his lips and kissed her wrist. "I never thanked you for helping me. I could've bled out on that deck."

"I never would've allowed that to happen." She cupped his face with her hand, tangling her fingers in his hair.

Rio dragged in a breath. "It's not that I don't want to protect you and Max. I'd go to the ends of the earth to do that."

"Just not Silverhill."

"I guess I don't have a choice now, do I?"

"You don't have to mingle with your brothers if you don't want. We can stay at my brother's ranch. I already called him to let him know we're on our way."

He ignored her reference to his *half* brothers. "It's your brother's ranch, not yours?"

"My parents had left it to both of us, but I sold out my share to Jared." She shrugged, but her stiff shoulders hinted at pain and regret.

"Sounds like you couldn't wait to get out of Silverhill. Why is it so important to return there now?"

"I told you before. Home and family became important to me only after I lost mine. Besides, it's the safest place I can think of. Everyone knows me there."

Including all those McClintocks.

"There is one problem with your timing." Rio raked his hands through his hair, catching his breath at the pain in his shoulder.

Tori blinked. "What's that?"

"It's ski season. I'm not that familiar with Silverhill, since I just visited the one time, but it looked like the place does a brisk business for skiers. Don't forget. That's how my mother met Ralph McClintock. She was a ski instructor, and I never knew a more rootless person than my mom."

The blank look on Tori's pretty face told him that the desire to return to her roots had blinded her to any other factors.

"Silverhill is going to be filled with strangers at this time of year, Tori. You're not going to recognize every face on the street. And that's an advantage for Alexi, not you."

She hugged herself as her face blanched. "Maybe the CIA will get Grant to talk about his association with Alexi. In the meantime, I guess that just means you're going to have to work harder to earn your money."

The fasten seatbelt sign pinged, and Derrick's voice scratched over the speaker. "We're coming in, folks."

Rio yanked up the shade and pressed his forehead against the cold window, gazing at the snowcapped Rockies. If the CIA couldn't stop Alexi Zherkov, the Mad Prince would know exactly where to look for Tori and Max. His reluctance to meet up with his half brothers represented only a sliver of his uneasiness at returning to Silverhill. His greater concern involved Tori and Max. Her decision to go home just put her life in danger.

TORI WANTED TO SMACK Jared's tight face. Had living in the mountains his entire life frozen his heart? Would he go on blaming her for their parents' deaths forever?

She settled in the backseat of Jared's Range Rover and pulled Max close, wrapping his oversize jacket around him. Rio slid in on the other side of Max and raised his brows. He must consider her crazy for wanting to return to her cold fish of a brother, but Rio wouldn't understand the pull of a place. He'd never experienced that with his mother. He never had a place to call home.

Jared adjusted his rearview mirror, making eye contact with Rio. "So you're really the long-lost McClintock brother? What are the odds of that? But leave it to my sister to drag one of the McClintocks into her mess. She always had one of those boys dancing to her tune, jumping in to save her."

Tori clenched her teeth. The only reason she'd decided to stay at the ranch was because Jared and his family were going away for Christmas. He hadn't changed a bit.

Rio narrowed his eyes. "As her brother, why didn't you jump in to save her?"

Jared's face reddened, and then he shook his head. "That'd be a full-time job, which you're about to discover."

"Lucky for me it is a full-time job." Rio reached across Max and squeezed Tori's thigh.

She grinned her thanks. It felt good to have Rio in her corner. She hoped he didn't swallow Jared's clumsy remarks about the McClintocks hook, line and sinker. Sure, they'd helped her out, but they'd helped out all their friends. Of course, maybe she'd had a few more troubles than the rest of their gang.

She'd watched Rio's face during Jared's diatribe, watched for the characteristic hardening of the jaw and the crease between his eyes every time someone mentioned his brothers. But he'd either gotten used to being compared to the rest of the McClintocks, or he'd learned to school his features into indifference.

She relaxed her shoulders and began pointing out landmarks to Max, who leaned across her lap to peer outside. "Pretty soon we'll be on Main Street. It's the busiest street in Silverhill and should be all decorated for Christmas."

"Is that where Cora and Derrick will be?"

"No, sweetie. Cora and Derrick are staying in Durango. They're going back to Hawaii."

"Are they going to see my father?"

A knife twisted in Tori's gut, and she exchanged a quick glance with Rio. She knew leaving Max with Alexi would have jeopardized Max's safety—maybe not today, not tomorrow, but somewhere down the line, one of Alexi's enemies would attempt to take out his revenge on Alexi by harming Max. But Max loved his father. Alexi had fostered an unhealthy relationship with Max, spoiling him and yet imposing a strict set of rules and regulations, unnatural for a little boy. In short, he had been grooming him to be Prince of Glazkova.

"I don't think Cora and Derrick know your father." She tousled his hair. "Your father is very busy right now."

Jared snorted. "That maniac's going to come after you, isn't he? I'm glad we'll be on vacation."

Rio jerked forward and clamped his hand on the side of Jared's seat. "Watch your mouth around the boy."

Jared coughed and grasped the steering wheel. "Sure."

Rio's fingers dug into the leather seat. "Apologize to your sister."

"Sorry, Tori."

"Whatever." A thrill of pleasure zinged through her veins. That's the first apology she'd ever heard from Jared, as insincere as it seemed. Rio had embraced his duties as her bodyguard and protector, and she felt that embrace all the way across the seat.

The big car swept down the hill and rolled onto Silverhill's Main Street. As she pointed out the Christmas decorations to Max, Tori's heart was sinking down to her toes.

The people. The crowds.

She gripped her hands in her lap. "Is it always this crowded now at this time of year?"

Jared answered, "Yeah. As some of the other ski resorts get more exclusive and more expensive, it drives people to Silverhill. Winter's worse, but summer's not much better these days. If Rod McClintock gets his way and sets up his dude ranch on his property and the Price property he got his hands on when he married Ennis Price's granddaughter, summer is going to be as packed as winter."

Tori sucked in her lower lip and slid a glance toward Rio. He'd been right. Alexi wouldn't have too much trouble slipping a couple of his goons into this winter mix. Slap a pair of ski boots on them and they'd blend right in.

Rio started questioning Jared about the ranch, the location, the entrances, the terrain and every other detail about it.

Tori sighed and kissed the top of Max's head. They'd be okay—not because she'd returned to Silverhill, but because she had a McClintock on her side…the right McClintock.

RIO COLLAPSED ON THE bed in the guest bedroom at the Scott ranch, folding his good arm beneath his head. When he'd met Tori's brother and got an earful of his barbs against her, he'd wondered why the heck she'd want to return to Silverhill. Then she'd begun telling Max about the countryside out the car window and sharing stories with him about her childhood. The warmth in her voice had sent an ache to the pit of Rio's stomach.

Despite her jerk of a brother's attitude toward her, Tori had come home. And she wanted to share this home with her son. The only thing his mother had wanted to share with him was the open road. He'd never even met his grandparents. They'd up and moved back to Mexico when his mother had run away from home as a teenager.

Children's shrieks blasted up the staircase and Rio dragged a pillow across his head. Tori had two nephews and a niece, and they were tearing around the house with their newfound cousin. Kids adapted so easily. Jared's three kids had accepted Max as one of their own, no questions asked.

What if he had met his half brothers when they'd all been Max's age or even older? Would they have accepted him? Offered him that familial bond?

His mother had never bothered coming back to Silverhill, even after the wife Ralph had cheated on with her had moved on. Ralph had known of Rio's existence. He'd proven that, after trying to turn that property over to him. Why hadn't his father come to steal him away in the middle of the night from his selfish, hedonistic mother?

He jumped at the rap on the door. Tori poked her head in the room. "Are you okay in here? Do you need some more rest? Dinner's going to be ready in about a half an hour if we can ever get those kids to settle down."

He perched on the edge of the bed. "I'm good. How are you feeling?"

She stretched her arms above her head and twirled into the room. "I feel great. I know my brother's an ass, but his wife's a sweetheart and I adore the kids. Are you going to the doctor tomorrow for your shoulder?"

"Yeah, but Cora and Derrick did a good job. I think I'm good to go. Give me a few minutes and I'll be right down. After dinner, I want your brother to give me a tour of the ranch. I want to scope out any weak spots."

Tori dropped her arms and wrapped them around her body. "I-it's going to be okay here, isn't it, Rio?"

He bounded from the bed and embraced her, pressing her body along every line of his. It seemed like forever since he'd held her in his arms. He brushed his lips against hers and whispered against her mouth, "I'll protect you."

She kissed him through her smile. "I know you will."

When Tori left the room, Rio went into the adjoining bathroom and splashed some water on his face. As he swiped a towel across his face, his cell phone rang in the bedroom. He checked the display and slid it open.

"Hey, Ted."

"How's the shoulder, man?"

Rio rolled his injured shoulder as if to check before answering Ted's question. "It's still there. No problems."

"Good, because you have other problems."

Rio's pulse ticked up a few notches. "Oh?"

"Mad Prince Alexi knows everything and he's coming for his son…and his ex-wife."

A FEW DAYS AFTER THEIR arrival, the silence of the house had Tori looking over her shoulder. She banged the cupboards in the kitchen as she got herself a snack just to hear the noise.

"Everything okay?" Rio poked his head into the kitchen, clutching his cell phone, a furrow between his brows.

"Everything's fine. Just a little too quiet without the kids." The tension eased out of her shoulders. She didn't have to worry with Rio in the next room jumping at every sound. Tugging the refrigerator door open, Tori asked, "You want something to drink?"

"Water." He wedged a shoulder against the partition between the kitchen and the family room. "You really miss your brother?"

She laughed and poured him a glass of cool water from the fridge. "He's amazingly pompous, isn't he? Still, I enjoyed seeing Max play with his cousins."

He took the glass from her hand, their fingers touching. It had been torture being in this house with Rio and keeping a cap on her feelings. She didn't want her brother weighing in on the inappropriateness of falling for your bodyguard, but Jared and his family had left for Florida this morning. There was nobody left to judge her, nobody left to keep her and Rio apart. Except Rio.

He took a long pull from the glass and set it down on the counter. "Tori, after Christmas, I think you and Max need to find another place to hide out from Alexi."

Her hand jerked, and her own water sloshed over the side of her glass. "I feel safe in Silverhill."

"He knows you took Max. Silverhill is the first place he'll look."

"He can look, but he can't touch. He's going to come after me with lawyers anyway until I can prove he's a dangerous criminal." She raised her chin. "We can protect Max here."

"For how long? Do you always want to be on your guard, afraid of the very silence?"

She banged her glass on the countertop. "I can't spend my life running and hiding. I've already spent the past two years on the move—trailing Alexi, hoping for glimpses of my son. Do something about Alexi. Arrest him."

"I wish we could. The local cops in Maui were able to charge Alexi's men with weapons violations, but they didn't have anything to pin on Alexi. He's more slippery than that ice frosting the sidewalk on Main Street."

"I'm staying here." She narrowed her eyes and leveled a finger at Rio. "It seems to me that I have more confidence in your abilities than you do."

A muscle ticked in his jaw, and his dark eyes flashed fire. He took a step toward her and stopped when someone banged on the front door.

Tori tripped back and grasped the handle of the refrigerator. Would it always be this way?

Rio held out his hand and crept to the office. The safety of his gun clicked while he inched toward the door and leaned against it. His chest rose and fell with every breath, and his coiled muscles looked ready to spring into action. He twitched the curtains at the window bordering the front door.

Tori held her breath, but Rio shook his head and stepped back. "It's for you."

Crinkling her brow, Tori crossed the room and peered out the window. She gave a shriek and flung open the front door, landing in the arms of Rafe McClintock, youngest McClintock brother and town sheriff.

Rafe hoisted her in his arms and staggered into the room where he swung her around. "You're heavier than I remember, or I'm getting old."

She smacked his shoulders with her open palms. "You're getting old."

"Where's your boy?"

"Max is upstairs sleeping. He's still recovering from our whirlwind escape from Maui."

Rafe kissed her square on the lips and handed her to his brother, Rod, standing silently in the doorway. Rod hugged her and pecked her cheek. "It's great to see you again, Tori."

She rubbed her knuckles along his lean jaw. "You, too. I heard you married Ennis Price's granddaughter. That must've broken hearts all across southern Colorado."

Rafe grinned. "Yeah, especially those hearts set on getting a piece of old Ennis's ranch, the Price Is Right."

Rod shot his younger brother a look that would turn most men to jelly, but Rafe shrugged it off and laughed.

Tori turned toward Rio, standing stiffly by the kitchen counter, tension radiating from his body in waves. Her hands flapped uselessly. "Your bro...umm...Rio's here."

Rafe launched forward, hand outstretched. "We heard you were in town. That's why we dropped by, although we wanted to wait until Tori's dry stick of a brother left." He pointed to Rio's weapon shoved in his waistband. "Not planning a little fratricide, are you?"

Rio clasped his brother's hand, his jaw tight. The clasp lasted a few beats longer than necessary, and Tori wondered if Rio was trying to squeeze the life out of Rafe. She turned to Rod to break the awkward silence, but he offered no help at all.

His eyes narrowed before he pushed off the doorjamb and sauntered toward Rio. "That land's still yours if you want it. I never filed the papers."

"Not interested." Rio shrugged.

Tori sucked in her lower lip, twisting her hands in front of her. This was not the happy reunion she'd hoped for. "Where's Ryder?"

Rafe grinned at his two brooding brothers. "Ryder

and Julia are coming in tomorrow. She just had a baby a few months ago. Did you know that?"

"Dana told me." She put her hand on Rio's arm. "Julia is Ryder's wife. They have an older daughter, too."

Rio's eyes flickered. "Is Dana the one who told you about Alexi going to Maui?"

Rio really knew how to ruin an already bad situation. "Yeah."

"You're here to protect Tori against her ex-husband?" Rod's gaze dropped to Tori's hand still resting on Rio's forearm.

"Yeah."

"I heard he's one crazy SOB. If you need any help, call us in." He jerked his thumb toward Rafe. "We'd do anything to protect Tori."

Rio plucked his weapon from his waistband and carefully placed it on the counter. Then he squared his shoulders. "Thanks for the offer, but I don't need any help protecting Tori."

"Then you don't know Tori."

"I know Tori...really well."

Tori rolled her eyes. This was turning into a pissing contest between these two stubborn men. Digging her fingers into Rio's arm, she reached over and grabbed Rod's hand. "I know I'll be safe with *all* the McClintocks on my side."

Rafe laughed and tugged her hair. "Well, you've got us. You're both joining us for Christmas, right? We're doing it McClintock-style at the ranch. Rod's wife Callie is an artist and she's been decorating and making everything pretty. The kids can't wait to meet Max."

Rio took a breath, but Tori beamed at Rafe and said, "Of course, we're coming. Those Christmas trees in Maui just looked all wrong."

"Is the old man going to be there?" Rio's harsh voice ripped through the laughter.

"He's too ill to travel." Rod disentangled his hand from Tori's and crossed his arms over his chest. "He and his wife, Pam, are in Palm Springs. You should fly out to pay him a visit one of these days. I mean, since he turned over that land to you and all."

"Maybe I will."

Rafe cut into the charged air, like he usually did. "Rio, if you have some time, I'd like to see the alarm system you installed. With the crowds in Silverhill growing bigger and bigger each winter, some of the business owners in town are looking into alarm systems."

Rio's nostrils flared, and Tori caught her breath. Was he going to refuse him?

Instead, he rolled his shoulders and said, "Sure, follow me."

Tori blew out a breath as the two men retreated to Jared's office, heads together as they discussed Rio's system. Rafe could usually get anyone to come around, even his prickly older brother.

She felt Rod's gaze burning a hole in the back of her head. She spun around. "What?"

"You two have a thing for each other, don't you?" He hooked his thumbs in his belt loop and rocked back on his heels.

Her mouth gaped open. Then she snapped it shut and scowled. "And why is that your business?"

"It's dangerous. When you care for someone, it muddies the waters, makes you act recklessly. Rio's a hothead, isn't he? He takes risks."

Tori pressed her fingers against her lips, keeping mum about Rio's actions—joining her at the hotel, slipping in with the catering staff, jumping up on the boat to fire at

Alexi's men. Yeah, he took risks, but every one of them had resulted in Max's escape.

"He's solid, Rod. He'd go to the ends of the earth to protect me and Max."

He shook his head. "I'm not doubting his loyalty or his skill set. It's clear he's a dangerous foe…and a deadly one. But when a man's heart is on the line, he can make some dumb choices."

"The fact that Rio lo…cares about me makes him more dedicated."

"Just call us if you need us, Tori…the other McClintock brothers."

Chapter Fifteen

Two more days until Christmas, and the McClintocks charged toward the holiday full-throttle. Seemed that family always did everything full-throttle. His family.

As a light snow dusted Rio's shoulders, he buckled Max into his booster seat in the back of Jared's Range Rover and slammed the door. He slid onto the passenger seat and hit the dashboard with his palm. "Let's go."

Shifting the car into reverse, Tori glanced sideways at him. "Don't worry. I know how to drive in snow."

"Do I look worried?"

"Yeah, you've had a furrow between your brows all day. I-is there something you haven't told me about you-know-who?" She glanced quickly into the backseat.

"I told you everything, Tori. He knows we took him, he probably knows you're here, and we haven't been able to arrest him yet." He didn't tell her the silence from Alexi's camp worried the hell out of him. If Alexi or one of his goons had come out to Silverhill by now, blustering and threatening, Rio could handle that. He could meet those threats head-on and with gusto.

Alexi was plotting and planning all right, but he was doing it in the dark. Whatever he had up his royal sleeve would take them by surprise.

Tori bit her lip as she edged the car down the drive.

"Something has to break soon. Maybe the CIA will discover his warehouse in Glazkova. In the meantime, let's just enjoy the holiday."

Rio stared out at the white landscape. He was almost as worried about Christmas with the McClintock clan as he was about Alexi. He'd gotten to know his brothers a little better in the past couple of days, and despite himself, he liked them, or at least respected them.

Who couldn't like Rafe? The sheriff's easygoing manner and sense of humor had everyone in town singing his praises and laughing at his jokes. Rod was harder to figure—taciturn, moody—heck, the guy reminded him of himself. And Ryder, who'd come into town with his gentle wife and daughter and newborn baby, had a mind like a steel trap. The bad guys were lucky Ryder wasn't in the field anymore, but he could probably do more damage behind his desk than twenty field ops.

Rio pressed his forehead against the cold glass. He'd given his half brothers a chance for Tori's sake. He'd pretty much do anything for her now and cursed his own weakness. He had to get her out of Silverhill. Maybe she needed to go into the Witness Protection Program until she was safe.

And when would that be? Not until Prince Alexi Zherkov was behind bars or dead.

"We're here." She swung to the curb in front of a brightly lit Mexican restaurant.

Rio rubbed the cold spot on his forehead and pulled on his gloves. "Just the three of us tonight, right? No other McClintocks are going to swagger in here and join us?"

She turned off the engine and sat clutching the steering wheel. "I thought you were getting along with your brothers."

"Half brothers," he said out of habit. "They're okay, I guess, but I want a night alone with you and Max."

Leaning over, she whispered in his ear, "You have me to yourself when the lights go out."

Her warm breath and sensuous tone, like sweet honey, made his blood pound hot and thick. Since her brother and his family had left, Rio had joined Tori in her bed every night after they'd tucked in Max. Then he'd creep back to his own room before dawn like a thief in the night.

Making love with Tori every night had dulled his sharp edges, filled him with lazy contentment. Put her and Max in danger. "About that…"

She put a gloved finger to his lips. "Stop. I need to curl up next to you at night, Rio. Without you in my bed, I'd be jumping at every snapping twig outside."

He bit back his protest and kissed the tip of her finger, the one she had him wrapped around with skill and ease. He couldn't say no to this woman.

Where would that land him when this all ended?

She grabbed the door handle, and he put out his hand. "Wait. You know the drill."

He slid from the car and scanned the pedestrians braving the snow. Fat, wet blobs smacked the side of his face, and he squinted against the cold. They'd come out to dinner early to avoid the big storm rolling in tonight, but it looked like the weather forecast had misjudged the timing.

Seeing nothing that set off his internal alarm, he poked his head in the car. "All clear."

Those two words sounded hollow and fake. All clear for now, but something nagged him, tugged at the edges of his consciousness. Tori had to get out of Silverhill, disappear in some random area of the country where her ex-husband would never find her. Disappear from his life.

Rio unbuckled Max from his booster and tucked him under one arm, carrying him into the restaurant. He raised his brows at the packed dining room. "Seems not even a blizzard can keep these people away. The food must be good."

Tori smiled at the hostess and requested a table for three. "Well, the food is good and the margaritas are legendary, but most people come here for the skiing and a little snow isn't going to deter them."

"A little snow?" He tipped his head toward the window. "I think that storm is rolling in earlier than predicted. Let's not stay too long."

She grabbed his hand, pressing her body against his arm. "I agree. Early bedtime for Max and a big blaze in the fireplace for us."

They wound up with a table in the corner and ordered two margaritas from the young waiter. When he asked them if they wanted to share a pitcher, Tori shook her head. "One's my limit on a night like this."

The waiter nodded his head. "That's smart. I worry about some of these tourists."

"Are you a local then?"

The young man's cheeks formed two spots of color. "Not exactly, but I've been working here the past two winters."

"Where are you from?" Rio spoke a couple of languages and could pick up accents quickly, and this kid had one from Eastern Europe.

Tapping his badge, the waiter smiled. "Czech Republic."

Rio peered at the badge pinned to the young man's shirt with his name and hometown etched into it. Like a lot of tourist locations, Silverhill attracted young people from all over the world.

"Your English is good, Tomas."

Tomas blushed on top of his blush and took their food orders, insisting they try the albondigas soup, his personal favorite.

While Max stuffed chips drenched in hot salsa into his mouth and Tori chattered on about local gossip, Rio watched the door. His gaze darted around the restaurant where laughing tourists, oblivious to the brewing storm, knocked back margaritas and tequila shots.

Maybe the timing had kicked his senses into over-drive, maybe the waiting, but he sensed Alexi was about to make his move. He'd want his son back with him in Glazkova for Christmas.

"Hello?" Tori tapped his knuckles with a fork. "You in there?"

He shifted his gaze back to her face, so bright and glowing with happiness. She had her son, and they'd made it back to Silverhill for Christmas. She couldn't see beyond that.

"I'm sorry." He dabbed her mouth with his napkin. "You have a little salt on your lip."

"You have that worried look again." She planted her elbows on the table. "We're perfectly safe. He's not going to snatch him in a public place. He's not going to waylay us on the drive back to my brother's ranch since he knows you're armed and lethal. And you've turned the ranch into a fortress. There's no way he's getting in there. He can't get to us."

Rio rolled his shoulders and pasted a false smile on his face. There were always ways to get to someone…if you knew their location.

By the time the soup came, Rio had ingested enough

salt from the rim of his glass and the chips and salsa to start his own mine. He finished half the bowl because Tomas, their waiter, kept asking them how they liked it, but he pushed the rest away.

Tori pointed at his bowl with her spoon. "Are you going to finish that?"

"You just don't want to disappoint Tomas, do you?"

She laughed. "He's so earnest. You can just imagine some babushka pinching his ruddy cheeks."

While Tori dipped into his remaining soup, Rio rubbed his eyes. *Babushka*. How had Alexi known that the CIA was planning to interrupt his drug deal with Grant Swain? Rio had made a mistake by infiltrating the catering staff and showing his hand. His uneasiness about Tori in that house had clouded his judgment. Would it happen again in Silverhill?

Hell, he was sleeping with the woman he was supposed to be protecting. A complete breach of his duties.

Tomas delivered the rest of their meal with a smile. "Did you enjoy the soup?"

"It was delicious. Even my son liked it, didn't you?" She tweaked Max's nose as he smashed his hundredth chip into his face.

Bet his old man never let him eat like that.

Rio picked at his dinner, trying to concentrate on Tori's words and automatically answering Max's nonstop questions. Thoughts of escape consumed him. They had to get away from Silverhill. The CIA could stash Tori and Max away in some nondescript town where she had no ties or connections. No friends or family. No him.

After Christmas. He'd convince her after Christmas. He could probably get her brother to work on her and maybe even his brothers…half brothers. She listened to them. She trusted them.

"I think we'd better head back." He shoved his plate away. "That storm is howling down on us now. How many years has it been since you've actually driven in this kind of weather?"

Yawning, Tori ducked her head to get a glimpse through the window. "It's been a few years. I think the food and the margarita just hit me. I'm tired."

"Do you want me to drive?" He waved Tomas over to their table. "We're ready for the check."

"No, I'm good to drive."

The storm blustered outside and rattled the windows of the restaurant where conversation stalled. Finally the tourists realized what Rio had seen coming all night. The blizzard had hit Silverhill early.

Maybe the weather had caused his sense of foreboding, but he planned to take the warning and run with it. He'd remove Tori from Silverhill after Christmas if he had to drug her and sling her over his shoulder to do it.

The restaurant began to empty, and Rio scanned the room for Tomas. He'd asked for that check ten minutes ago. "Do you see our waiter?"

Tori waved her hand toward the kitchen. "He's been flitting around over there."

"Next time you see him, get his attention. We need to leave—now."

Tori's smile froze on her face. "You mean leave the restaurant."

"For now, leave the restaurant."

"And for later?" She stifled a yawn, although her eyes brightened to alertness.

"That's for later." He snapped his fingers as Tomas swung out of the kitchen. "Tomas, the check, please."

The young waiter clapped a hand over his mouth and

scurried to the register. He rushed back to the table, waving their bill in front of him. "I'm sorry. With the snow coming down outside, we had to arrange transportation for some of our customers."

Rio slapped down some cash. "Keep it."

"Thank you, and drive safely."

Tori scooped up Max from his seat and stumbled back. "Oops. Could you take him, Rio? He's getting so heavy and I don't want him walking out there in the snow."

Rio zipped up his jacket and took Max from Tori's arms while he shook off a yawn. Mexican food had a soporific effect on him, too. The damn stuff just sat in your belly.

Tori bundled into her coat, tugged on her gloves and fished her keys out of her purse. Then she spent five minutes thanking the owners, whom she'd known since childhood, and praising Tomas.

The restaurant owner pinched Max's cheek and patted Tori's arm. "Are you okay to drive, Tori? I know our margaritas pack a powerful punch."

"I know that, too. That's why I had just one. Have a merry Christmas, and we'll send Rafe over tomorrow to pick up some tamales for Christmas Eve."

The woman tapped her temple. "Very smart. We always give the sheriff a special deal."

Finally they staggered outside, and the snow pelted their faces. The icy sharpness needled Rio's flesh, momentaily reviving him after the warm, stuffy restaurant. He secured Max, already sleepy, into his booster seat as Tori hopped into the front seat, rubbing her gloved hands.

Rio scraped the windows before climbing into the Range Rover next to her. The car had all-wheel drive and could handle the roads, and Tori assured him she could make the drive blindfolded. With the white curtain descending all around them, she'd have to make good on that promise.

Tori cranked up the heat and as soon as Rio settled into his warmed seat and reclined against the headrest, his limbs felt heavy and languorous. He rubbed a circle against the fogged window and peered out at the multicolored lights lining Main Street.

As soon as they pulled onto the roadway leading to the ranch, Rio's lids tugged down over his eyes.

Tori murmured, "I'm so tired. It must be the snow."

"Or the heat." Rio shook his head and dialed down the heater.

The big SUV plowed through the snow, and then began to drift toward the side of the road. Rio's brain clicked, but his tongue couldn't form the words of warning on his lips. As if in slow motion, he nudged Tori's arm.

She jerked awake, and the steering wheel jerked with her. The car veered back into its lane. "I can't stay..."

Tori's head dropped to the side, and the car wandered across the dividing line. Luckily, no other cars were braving the road tonight, and the Range Rover was beginning to slow down as Tori's foot slipped from the accelerator.

If Rio could just rouse himself from his own stupor, he could take the wheel and steer them to safety. But the prospect of even raising his arm to grab the steering wheel proved too daunting for his languid muscles to accomplish.

Through his foggy brain, one word pounded—*why, why, why?* Why were they both so tired? His eyes drifted shut again, and his head lolled to the side just as the

Range Rover crawled to a stop, bumping a guardrail at the side of the road.

Thank God.

Rio pressed his cheek against the cold window. If he could get out, he'd revive himself in the snow.

Headlights flooded the car and Rio's hand fell open, releasing the door handle he'd been trying to pull. Someone was here to help.

Why, why, why?

The words pierced through his muddled brain again. This couldn't be natural. A bright light flashed in his head. *Someone had drugged them.*

He struggled against the darkness sliding across his mind, inch by inch. His battle to keep it at bay got an unexpected boost when someone yanked open the driver's side door, flooding the car with light and freezing cold.

Rio peeled one eye open. Two men crowded the doorway, and the smell of tobacco revived him even more. He tried to control his slack mouth to ask for help, but before he could one of the men spoke…in Russian.

"Are they out?"

"Looks like they're out cold…in a manner of speaking."

The other man guffawed, and Max stirred and whimpered in the back seat.

Rio immediately shut his one functioning eye. If they thought he was out, he'd accommodate them.

"Prince Maksim is awake."

The back door of the car jerked open, and Mad Prince Alexi whispered, "My son, my son."

As buckles snapped and Max's jacket crinkled, Rio concentrated all his efforts on moving one finger. He couldn't do it. Alexi was stealing Max right from under his nose, and he couldn't do a damned thing to stop him.

"And the princess?"

"Take her."

Alexi's words punched Rio in the gut, and hot rage coursed through his mind, but not his body, which remained on vacation.

More snaps and rustling amid Max's whining. "Is Mommy sleeping?"

"Yes, my son. She's very tired, but we're going to bring her back to Glazkova with us. We're going to be a family again."

Rio yelled, "Over my drugged body," but the words remained imprisoned in his head.

A sliding noise and Rio could no longer feel the warmth of Tori's body in the next seat. They had her.

Max sniffled. "What about Rio? We're supposed to have Christmas."

"We will have our own Christmas in Glazkova, my son, my prince."

The back door slammed shut, and Max's cries became fainter. The cold air still whooshed inside the car from the driver's side, and Rio held on to one corner of his consciousness. He had to discover where Alexi was taking them.

Bodies again pressed against the driver's side of the car. The smell of tobacco, booze and garlic kept Rio awake, and he breathed in the mingled odors like a smelling salt.

"What about him, Prince Alexi?"

The other man grunted. "Shoot him. He's a filthy CIA collaborator."

"No." Alexi spoke sharply. "Tomas said McClintock finished that bowl of soup. He should have enough dope in him to keep him out for several more hours. He won't know what hit him and by the time he wakes, if he wakes, we'll be secure in our hideout until this miserable weather clears and we can take off."

"Why not just off him so he can't come after us again?"

"The CIA won't care about a family dispute over custody. They've proven that time and again. But killing one of their top independent contractors? They'd never stop coming after me. Leave him. Maybe he'll die of hypothermia. The CIA can't blame me for that."

A big hand grabbed Rio's forearm, and for a split second he thought Alexi had changed his mind. Then the hand threw Rio's arm to the side and burrowed into his pocket. Not finding what he was seeking, Alexi's thug reached across Rio's body to the other pocket and scooped out his cell phone.

Someone sank into the driver's seat, and the SUV rolled down the embankment, sinking into the soft carpet of snow. They planned to leave him here to die.

Leaving all the doors open, the man clambered back to the road, his boots crunching the snow. The cold air splashed Rio's cheeks and soaked into his skin. If he didn't move, and soon, he'd freeze to death. He blinked his eyes and forced his fingers to move.

I didn't drink as much of that soup as Tomas thought, you SOB.

As the other truck roared to life, Rio groaned and reached across the seat in a futile effort to rescue the woman he loved.

Several minutes later, with the cold wind blasting his face and ripping through his body, Rio stretched his arms and legs as he awakened back to the land of the living. He staggered from the car and scooped up handfuls of snow, warming it into water between his gloved hands. He began drinking the cold water, filling his belly to bursting. Then he leaned forward and shoved two fingers down his throat. He retched and vomited into the scrubby bushes by the side of the road.

Whatever Tomas had slipped them in the soup was fast-acting, but Rio could make sure no more of the drug insinuated itself into his bloodstream. He threw up once more, his gut clenching into a spasm.

Then he grabbed more snow and rubbed it all over his face. Stamping his feet, he waved his arms above his head to get his circulation pumping at a normal rate.

At least this storm would keep Alexi on the ground and close by, giving Rio an opportunity to find them. If Alexi took Tori to Glazkova, Rio would never see her again. The Zherkovs practically owned that country. The Mad Prince could do anything he wanted to Tori, and he'd continue to endanger Max's life.

No. Rio would never allow that to happen.

He hauled himself up the embankment and onto the road. Squatting next to the tire tracks on the road, he poked at the pieces of his cell phone crushed beneath the tire of Alexi's car. He squinted into the snow-covered night. They'd headed north, nothing but wilderness that way. Of course, they wouldn't want to stay in Silverhill, and they couldn't get through to Durango. The storm he'd cursed hours ago now became Rio's best friend.

But he couldn't go wandering into the mountains in a blizzard. He'd probably end up walking off the edge of a cliff. Alexi obviously had a plan. He'd planted Tomas here for a couple of years as insurance, and that policy had just paid off. Tomas had already scoped out a hiding place, a backup plan. Alexi had called it their *hideout*.

Rio didn't know the first thing about this terrain. But he knew who did.

Fully revived, Rio tucked his chin to his chest, folded his hands beneath his armpits and strode up the roadway. After ten minutes of walking on a couple of frozen sticks he used to call legs, he spied a revolving yellow light in the distance. He lurched to the side of the road. If Alexi had made a U-turn to check up on him, he'd lose his one chance of finding Tori and Max.

The grating noise of the vehicle preceded Rio's ability to determine its shape or size. But as the wide-load behemoth drew almost abreast of him, a surge of relief coursed through his chilled body. Snowplow to the rescue.

Rio stepped in front of the vehicle, waving his arms like a lunatic. The snowplow ground to a stop, and a bundled-up figure with just his eyes showing leaned out of the door.

"What are you doing out here?"

Waving his arm behind him, Rio yelled back, "My car stalled out on me. Can you turn around and take me to the McClintock ranch?"

The man pulled his hood farther over his face. "The McClintocks? What do you want with the McClintocks?"

Rio stepped into the light. "I'm Rio McClintock, they're my half…my brothers."

"Right. I heard you were in town." He shoved his hand into the pocket of his jacket and pulled out a phone. "I'm just going to give them a call. Small town, you know. We look after our own."

Rio held a frosty breath. Would his brothers turn their backs on him now? What right did he have to expect anything from them? No. They'd at least help Tori. They'd do anything to help Tori.

After a brief conversation on the phone, the driver said, "Hop on in."

Fifteen minutes later, the snowplow lumbered its way up the long drive to Rod McClintock's ranch, clearing the path as it went forward. Jumping from the vehicle, Rio thanked the man and then bounded up the front steps.

The door swung open before Rio even reached the porch. Warmth and laughter spilled from the house, and lights glowed a cheerful welcome. In another time— there was nothing cheerful about the news he brought.

Rafe propped up the door with his shoulder, Rod and Ryder crowding in behind him. Rafe's smile faded as he took in Rio's solitary form. "What's going on? Where are Tori and Max?"

Rio heaved himself up the last step, his jaw tight, the backs of his eyes aching with cold. "Alexi took them and I need your help."

SOMETHING PINCHED HER inner arm, and Tori tried to swat it away, but rough hands cinched her wrist and upper arm, holding her still.

Tori moaned and shifted on the hard earth. When her captor released her arm, she rubbed the sore spot on the inside of her elbow. Her head pounded with drumbeats of pain and her tongue stuck to the roof of her dry mouth. Max whimpered near her ear, his soft, sleepy body burrowing into hers.

She curled an arm around him and struggled to sit upright. A man holding a syringe backed into the semicircle around the fire and collapsed next to his weapon. Her gaze shifted from one man to the next, resting on

Alexi front and center. The restaurant and then sleep, encroaching, mind-numbing sleep.

She licked her lips, hugging Max tighter. They'd been drugged. And drugged again—she glanced at the pinprick in her arm. Her gaze darted around the dark, hollow cave as terror seeped into her bones. What had they done with Rio?

Alexi tsked. "Looking for your boyfriend? Don't bother. He's dead."

His words sucked the air from her lungs, and she doubled over, resting her chin on Max's curls. Oh, God, she'd done this to Rio. She'd lured him into her dangerous world, bound him to her, all the while knowing Alexi would never relinquish his son. But what did he want with her?

She blinked her dry eyes and raised her head. "Tomas? The soup?"

Alexi rubbed his hands. "Prescient of me, wasn't it? I knew you'd head back to this godforsaken land one of these days, and I wanted to keep my options open."

She gulped. "How'd you know? How'd you time it for this night?"

He lifted his shoulders, uncharacteristically clad in a heavy down jacket, lined with fur, of course. "I didn't. But I knew you'd make it to that restaurant eventually. All the locals do, don't they? I'm always ready for anything, Victoria. You should know that by now."

Rio dead.

She shoved the thought from her brain, buried it in her consciousness to take out and examine later. She still had a chance to escape. The blizzard had grounded Alexi's operation and ruined his plans.

"What was in that syringe?"

"Just a little something to revive you, or you would've been out for a long time."

She almost wished that all-encompassing sleep had her in its grip. "What am I doing here? I figured you'd come for Max, but why me?"

"So many questions." Alexi poured himself a cup of hot coffee from a steaming thermos, the smell of the brew turning Tori's already unsettled stomach.

"My dear, you've become a loose cannon out in the big, bad world by yourself—following me, bothering my staff, working with the CIA. I think it's time for you to return home. You'll be safe and secure in Glazkova."

Panic roared through her body, shooting her full of adrenaline. Her leg jerked. "I'm not going back."

"You will." He blew on his coffee. "You won't ever leave Maksim again. And if that weren't motivation enough, I'm simply going to drug you up and load you on my private jet."

Tori forced her lips into a stiff smile. "Not going to happen."

Alexi shook his head, almost sadly. "This storm is supposed to wear itself out by tomorrow. We'll spend the night in this cozy cave and head for the plane tomorrow before anyone even realizes you're gone."

"Someone will find my brother's car on the side of the road. They'll find Rio's...Rio." She ended on a sob. The McClintocks would come after her. They'd find her and avenge their brother's death.

Alexi threw his head back and laughed. "The car is down an embankment, probably covered with two feet of snow by now and McClintock's body is a Popsicle."

Rage boiled her blood. She'd kill him with her bare hands. She shifted Max's body from her lap and rolled the blanket around him, tucking the ends around his chin.

She rose to her haunches and scooted closer to the fire in the center of the cave. She knew their location. Hell, if you grew up in Silverhill and had make-out sessions with the opposite sex, you had intimate knowledge of the caves.

Her muscles tensed, ready for anything. Alexi's two henchmen had weapons, but they lay carelessly on the ground by crossed legs. She'd bet one planned to guard her at night, at gunpoint, but with everyone wide awake now, except Max, they'd gotten lazy.

She liked lazy. She knew how to take advantage of lazy.

Alexi tipped more coffee into his cup and poured another. "Coffee, Victoria? It's going to be a long, cold night."

She held out her hand, trying to control the trembling. This might be her last act against her ex-husband, but she doubted the goons to her right would shoot her. Alexi didn't want her dead. God help her, he wanted her as his wife again. She could see the twisted desire in his obsidian eyes.

As Alexi extended his arm, the cup of hot coffee in his hand, Tori clenched her fist and smacked it against the cup. Alexi spewed a litany of Russian curse words as the liquid scalded his hand. The men jumped up, and then the ceiling of the cave seemed to crash in.

Four men dropped into the middle of the cave, and Tori rolled her body over Max's, peeking over her shoulder at the chaos unfolding. Rod struggled with one of the men, finally smacking him on the back of the head with the butt of his gun. Ryder had already subdued his man with a chokehold, and the man slithered to the floor, unconscious. Rafe had positioned himself at the cave's entrance, weapon aloft, securing the area.

And Rio. Rio! He and Alexi grappled on the cave floor until a gunshot echoed through the caverns. Tori gasped and covered her ringing ears. Her gaze locked on to the two figures. One peeled away from the other.

Rio lurched to his knees, holding his shoulder. Then he scuffled to her side wrapping his arms around her and an awakening Max. Tori pressed Max's face against her side and buried her own in Rio's wet jacket.

"I thought…he told me…" She couldn't finish the thought that had ripped her apart, darkened her world forever.

"Shh." He kissed her hair while he rubbed circles on her back. "He left me for dead, but remember? I never finished that soup. How'd you wake up so quickly? I figured we'd find you unconscious."

"Alexi gave me something to revive me. He just had to gloat. Is he…?"

Ryder dropped Alexi's arm and nodded, running a zipper across his lips and pointing to Max.

"I think he's drifting off again. He had some of our soup. We need to get him to the hospital."

Rafe burst through the cave opening, waving his gun. "Everything secure? Are there any more, Tori?"

"I didn't see any. What are you going to do with these two?" She gestured to the two men laid out on the cave floor.

"The Agency will pick them up, but you need to lock them up tonight, bro."

Rod unraveled a length of rope. "We need to revive them to march them out of here. I sure as hell am not going to carry them out of the mountains."

Rio pushed to his feet and helped Tori to hers, taking a dozing Max from her arms.

A shudder coursed through her body. Alexi dead. Her

nightmare had just ended in the caves of Silverhill. She placed her hand over Rio's heart and even beneath the layers of his jacket, shirt and long underwear she could still feel its steady beat.

"How'd you know? How'd you find me here?"

Rio jerked his thumb toward the three men rousing the prisoners and tying them together for the trek out of the mountains, the mountains they knew like an old familiar friend. "My brothers showed me the way."

Epilogue

Rio brushed the pad of his thumb across Tori's cheek as she blinked back tears watching Max rip into his biggest present under the tree. A present from the McClintock brothers.

Max dragged a saddle out of the box and shrieked above the already deafening sound of the other McClintock kids tearing wrapping paper and demolishing boxes. Rod's boy, Jesse, crawled to Max on his hands and knees nudging Ryder's little girl, Shelby, out of the way to have a look at Max's big gift. Rafe's daughter, Kelsey, the oldest of the brood, looked on with a superior smirk on her face.

Their mothers, Callie, Dana and Julia, clustered on the sofa, cooing over Julia and Ryder's newborn baby boy.

Max lugged the saddle to his mother. "Can I ride a horse now, Mommy?"

She stroked a curl out of his eye. "Well, someone has to teach your first. You can't just go jumping on a horse, even with a brand-new saddle."

Max turned his green eyes on Rio. "Can you teach me, Rio?"

Rafe erupted in laughter. "You're going to have to find a better teacher than Rio, son."

Rio clenched his jaw momentarily until he met his brother's bright blue gaze. He grinned and ruffled Max's hair. "Rafe is right, Max. I think your best bet is Rod 'cuz I heard Rafe is reckless and irresponsible."

This time Rod laughed as Rafe's mouth hung open. "You got that right, but don't let it get out. He's the sheriff of Silverhill, you know."

"Help me out here, bro." Rafe turned to Ryder who had plucked his son from his wife's arms and was dabbing drool from the baby's mouth.

Ryder skewered Rod with a piercing look. "Talk about reckless. At least Rafe met his wife in high school. Rod picked his up by the side of the road, already wearing a wedding dress."

Callie jumped from the sofa and draped her arms around Rod's shoulders. "Hey, that's totally uncalled for. He was just living up to the McClintock code—protect, serve and rescue."

"Yeah, and at least he does it here at home instead of in fifty different countries around the world." Rafe leveled an accusing finger at Ryder.

"You're attacking a man holding a baby? Why are you on me anyway? I just nailed Rod for you since you're still too scared of him to do it yourself."

Rio's shoulders relaxed as he watched his brothers' interactions. He knew they fought. He'd heard about some of their disagreements. But it all came back to this—the camaraderie among brothers.

And they had extended that to him. Sure, he knew rescuing Tori and Max had fueled their motivation for helping out the other night, but they hadn't hesitated for one second. Once Rio had given them the direction of Alexi's truck, they'd known immediately where he had headed…and they'd known how to get there.

Rio had formulated the rescue plan and they had listened. They hadn't tried to tell him to remain behind, even though his presence on the trek could've endangered them all. They'd respected the fact that Rio had to be the one to save Tori and Max. They'd respected him.

He nuzzled Tori's ear. "Are they always like this?"

She curved her hand around his neck. "Yeah, you'll get used to it if you stick around."

He ran a finger along the crease between her brows. They hadn't discussed the future. Max had been too sleepy to remember much of anything. They'd convinced him that his father had come around to say goodbye because he was ill and had to go away to get better. The CIA had taken custody of Alexi's two thugs, and they'd notified the State Department of the Prince of Glazkova's death.

Glazkova would fly his body home and give him a royal funeral with honors. Alexi's cousin would take over the reins of the little country. Rio hoped he didn't have the same criminal intent as the rest of the royal family because Glazkova's throne would belong to Maksim Zherkov one of these days.

Rio's gaze tracked around the room. A family…a big family with roots. It's all he'd ever dreamed of as a kid. Then he glanced into Tori's green eyes, clouded with questions and uncertainties.

"You will get used to it, won't you?"

He bent down and kissed her mouth. "Right now, I just want to get used to you."

She smiled beneath his lips and weaved her fingers through his hair to pull him closer. Brothers were handy, but he found all he'd ever dreamed of in Tori's kiss.

* * * * *

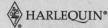
INTRIGUE

COMING NEXT MONTH

Available January 11, 2011

#1251 BRANDISHING A CROWN
Cowboys Royale
Rita Herron

#1252 THE TEXAS LAWMAN'S LAST STAND
Texas Maternity: Labor and Delivery
Delores Fossen

#1253 TWILIGHT WARRIOR
Long Mountain Heroes
Aimée Thurlo

#1254 GUNS AND THE GIRL NEXT DOOR
Mystery Men
HelenKay Dimon

#1255 MOUNTAIN MIDWIFE
Cassie Miles

#1256 SOLID AS STEELE
43 Light Street
Rebecca York

HICNM1210

REQUEST YOUR FREE BOOKS!

2 FREE NOVELS
PLUS 2
FREE GIFTS!

HARLEQUIN®
INTRIGUE®

Breathtaking Romantic Suspense

HARLEQUIN®

A Romance

FOR EVERY MOOD™

Spotlight on

Classic

Quintessential, modern love stories
that are romance at its finest.

See the next page
to enjoy a sneak peek from
the Harlequin Presents® series.

Harlequin Presents® is thrilled
to introduce the first installment of
an epic tale of passion and drama by
USA TODAY *Bestselling Author*
Penny Jordan*!*

When buttoned-up Giselle first meets
the devastatingly handsome Saul Parenti,
the heat between them is explosive....

"LET ME GET THIS STRAIGHT. Are you actually suggesting that I would stoop to that kind of game playing?"

Saul came out from behind his desk and walked toward her. Giselle could smell his hot male scent and it was making her dizzy, igniting a low, dull, pulsing ache that was taking over her whole body.

Giselle defended her suspicions. "You don't want me here."

"No," Saul agreed, "I don't."

And then he did what he had sworn he would not do, cursing himself beneath his breath as he reached for her, pulling her fiercely into his arms and kissing her with all the pent-up fury she had aroused in him from the moment he had first seen her.

Giselle certainly *wanted* to resist him. But the hand she raised to push him away developed a will of its own and was sliding along his bare arm beneath the sleeve of his shirt, and the body that should have been arching away from him was instead melting into him.

Beneath the pressure of his kiss he could feel and taste her gasp of undeniable response to him. He wanted to devour her, take her and drive them both until they were equally satiated—even whilst the anger within him that she should make him feel that way roared and burned it resentment of his need.

She was helpless, Giselle recognized, totally unable to withstand the storm lashing at her, able only to cling to the man who was the cause of it and pray that she would survive.

Somewhere else in the building a door banged. The sound exploded into the sensual tension that had enclosed them, driving them apart. Saul's chest was rising and falling as he fought for control; Giselle's whole body was trembling.

Without a word she turned and ran.

Find out what happens when Saul and Giselle succumb to their irresistible desire in

THE RELUCTANT SURRENDER

Available January 2011 from Harlequin Presents®